GADLY PLAIN

D1377598

GADLY PLAIN

A NOVEL

J. Michael Dew

CLADACH
Publishing

Gadly Plain: A Novel
Copyright © 2013 by J. Michael Dew
Published by:
Cladach Publishing
Greeley, Colorado 80633
www.cladach.com

All rights reserved.

Illustrations by Raw Spoon. More information about the artist
can be found at www.rawspoon.com.
Front cover photos: iStock Photo
Printed in the U.S.A.

Library of Congress Cataloging-in-Publication Data:
Dew, J. Michael, 1974-
   Gadly Plain : a novel / by J. Michael Dew.
      pages cm
   ISBN-13: 978-0-9818929-9-3
   ISBN-10: 0-9818929-9-X
   I. Title.
   PS3604.E894G33 2013
   813'.6--dc23
      2013008747

For my daughters:
Angelica Harriet, Gabriela Jean, and Marianna Sarita
so that they will always know the love of their father.

–J. Michael Dew

To Mom,
who organized art shows for my pictures
of things like sharks eating cars
and got our neighbors to come see them.

I wish you could see this.

Ross
(Raw Spoon)

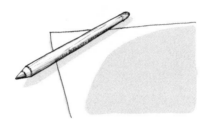

"I saw heaven standing open and there before me was a white horse whose rider is called Faithful and True."

–Revelation 19:11

I

There had been far worse chasms of despair throughout the history of the world—more gripping, suffocating, more inexplicably woeful—but Spring-baby Westbay couldn't imagine any such chasm because she had fallen into one of her very own. It could hardly have been helped. She was only twelve, and her dad had been dying for so long in Spring-baby's tiny memory that when he finally did pass away, miles from home and rebuke, in a hospital for veterans in Richmond, Virginia, the gravity of no more-ness weighed upon the girl with such sudden potency that sorrow had become the sole stuff of her limited existence.

Sorrow bullied her, kept her wilted, sober. Sorrow had come with a phone call from her grandfather on a brilliant day in June when school had just let out for the summer.

"Mom," she muttered after the screen door thwapped shut behind her. "What's wrong? What happened?"

Spring-baby's mother stood sobbing into the phone, grief strangling every word she tried to get out. Her own mother stood next to her.

"Gramma?"

"Your dad," her grandmother answered through tears of her own. "The new heart was fine, but his system was too weak. He died on the operation table. He coded, they call it."

Spring-baby watched her grandmother gently take the phone away, heard her say into it, "Okay. Okay now. We'll call you back in a bit. Spring-baby just walked in. I know. So young." She hung up, extended her hands.

That was all. There was nothing more. Spring-baby had already fallen away, letting the screen door make the announcement with another abrupt *thwap.*

She had plenty of places to run but nowhere really to go. The misshapen plot of ground on which her modest home stood ended where another plot picked up, for she lived in a borough in rural Pennsylvania with other houses and other children—Appalachian foothills compressing her little universe like earthen bookends. Eight seventeen north main street was the book she knew best. It was where she ate and colored, where she shared a bedroom with her little brother, Troy; it was the place around which she rode her banana seat bicycle, sometimes with a playing card flicking the spokes, sometimes not. Until the day she discovered that systems could fail and daddies could die, the world for Spring-baby was as aromatic as paste, as warm as winter nights always had been.

But she had never before seen her mother cry with such brokenness, such misery. She had witnessed her dad throw up into the toilet—once he even gestured her away as the sick gushed from his mouth—but what vomit truly had meant had been remote compared to the something beneath her bed whose unspeakable plans she thwarted time and again with every desperate leap.

So she ran through and across the backyards of at least four neighbors before finality like the bogeyman caught up with her at last and gobbled her up. Spring-baby cried herself parched, her face mercilessly continuing to wring itself dry long after the last tear had dripped from her chin. Then she found her way back home where extended family members had already begun to arrive and walked indoors to be pitied.

"Your daddy was a good man," they said. "He was so young, so young. Just thirty-three with two kids and a wife."

They squeezed her shoulders, smoothed back her dirty blonde hair: "Your daddy loved you so."

And though she nodded to agree, she was sure she couldn't be seen through the sadness that engulfed her. It was as if Spring-baby were dead, too, and the funeral she and her mother would attend ten hours away in the far-flung Kentucky town of her father's youth was also her funeral: the dead saying goodbye to the dead.

The day before they left, Spring-baby was outfitted for her interment: a black K-mart dress and black shoes to match. Troy got a squirt gun. Because he was five and Spring-baby's grandmother didn't think it prudent to expose one so young to a moment so unfathomable, it was decided that he stay with her in a little house on a hill she had shared with her husband going on forty years.

"He's too young to understand," she said. "It's Spring-baby that needs to be there."

And so Spring-baby went and was.

Her mother, Lorelei, chain-smoked Kool 100s from their home in Pennsylvania through Ohio and right into Kentucky, holding the cigarette by the partly rolled-down window so the rushing air would whisk away the smoke. The radio was on but neither mother nor daughter really paid it any attention. The journey of a day was understandably bleak even though the sky remained clear and the traffic, light. Spring-baby sat quietly on the passenger side of their dirty brown station wagon, gazing through the blur. They stopped for gas just twice. They ate their McDonald's on the road.

Eventually, Spring-baby remembered her dad had smelled of leather and Old Spice: musky invincibility, a scent like a fingerprint. It was what clung to her after she buried her head into the nape of his neck to say goodnight; it was the morphine that gently tugged her into her dreams.

For a man of unimpressive stature, he had the presence, so felt Spring-baby, of endless possibility, even when the medication conspired with the sickness, sinking his cheeks and paling his skin. He made Spring-baby and her brother laugh until their stomachs hurt, sometimes doing Daffy Duck, a cartoon dog, a feisty horse; it didn't matter. When she or her brother would yell, "Do the one! Do the one!" the character that would come alive in spite of work, then illness, then a futile stare-down with death, struck giddy chords that reverberated long after the show was over in how Spring-baby and her brother in imitation after her would try to do the one for themselves.

Spring-baby would grow to rely on those echoes, vainly attempting a throaty duck or an unbroken horse as her dad would spend more time removed and pensive, oftentimes on the back porch with nothing more than a forgotten cigarette and the virus that wouldn't go away. Because Troy hadn't known the characters as long as Spring-baby, he could never sense his dad's loneliness let alone the meaning of those quiet vigils.

Only once did Spring-baby hear her dad speak of going home to Kentucky and that was to her mother during a conversation in which even Spring-baby as she eavesdropped could tell that the words were sprinkled with longing.

"I want to go home," he said. "This is your home, but it isn't mine. I'm the one that's sick."

"But there's me, Mike. There's the kids."

"I know. I know," he stammered. "But I didn't think I was going to die."

And because Spring-baby had never been acquainted with death, couldn't possibly reach outside the boundaries of her own beautiful myopia, she, too, had been unable to sense the real depth of his loneliness: why he would eventually step off the back porch and hitchhike to his boyhood home and the safety of his parents' arms, why he would forsake the only life Spring-baby ever knew for the memory of the life he himself once had. Her observation from the back door she was forbidden to open stopped at Dad wanting time for Dad.

When he rested, it was no different. Only when she was told to do so could she open the door to her parents' simple bedroom and invade her father's repose. Increasingly, though, he lived asleep, so the times were rare when Spring-baby and sometimes her brother were allowed to rouse their father awake by bouncing on the mattress as he lay in the temporary sanctuary of dormancy.

"Not now," her mother would chide. "Your father's tired. Go outside and play."

Spring-baby, being the compliant child she was, would always release the doorknob and obey.

Yet the fantasy of disobeying was what consumed her now as she and her mother pressed through the new Kentucky night on narrow, winding roads crowded in by vegetation that buzzed and peeped. The lightning bugs in the periphery were like terrestrial stars that blinked green. The window openings were reduced to whistling slivers to ward off the cooling air. And on and on as the night grew ripe, Spring-baby turned the doorknob and pushed, turned and pushed, turned, pushed while her mother next to her continuously tried on and refitted "widow" like a prosthetic limb.

When they reached the budget motel where they were to

lay their heads, for Spring-baby's Kentucky grandparents could not accommodate any more bereavement besides their own, Lorelei and Spring-baby were just a half mile or so from the Nelson-Blick Funeral Home, a fitful night from the service, and now squarely underneath the dizzying reality that pressed them without mercy into the red Kentucky ground.

With a moroseness foreign to most her age, Spring-baby followed her mother to the room under the flickering, pale yellow light of exposed fluorescent bulbs.

"Let's get settled and go straight to bed," Lorelei said, unlocking the dented door. "Tomorrow will be a long day. Today was long enough."

The two shared a queen-sized bed. Old Spice and leather, for Spring-baby, were there to greet her instead of send her off. As for Lorelei, she clutched a musty pillow and cried herself to sleep, sending pathetic tremors across the sunken mattress until, it seemed, tremors were all there were in the vast, black world.

The viewing would begin at eleven the next morning. The immediate family was to be there thirty minutes prior. Lorelei was up before Spring-baby, vigorously taking the lint brush to a faded cotton dress. She let Spring-baby drowse as she drained the last sip of coffee from a lipstick-stained Styrofoam cup. She had retrieved the coffee along with a few dry muffins from the lobby.

"Spring-baby," Lorelei beckoned, rubbing her daughter's bare leg. "Time to get up. There's a muffin there on the dresser."

Spring-baby rolled and readjusted and whined herself awake before she swung her thin legs over the side of the bed and touched her feet to the floor.

"What kind?" she asked.

The rap on the door left the question unanswered.

"Room service!"

Spring-baby scurried to the door and opened it before her mother could register the intrusion.

"Spring-baby!" was all Lorelei could manage before the door swung open to reveal a sturdy-looking woman wearing a broad white apron, standing in front of a utility cart out of which poked dusters, toilet paper, a broom, a mop, and sundry bottles containing colored liquids.

"Good morning," the maid said with a detectable German accent. "Am I too early?" She smiled warmly. Her bobbed, gray-streaked hair reflected the morning sun.

"Well," Lorelei began. "If you could—"

"My dad died. We're getting ready to go see him. What it's called is a viewing."

Spring-baby was standing before the maid clothed in nothing more than panties and a t-shirt, yet her proclamation managed to make her starker than she already was.

Just then the maid clicked her tongue twice, reached into her apron pocket, and pulled out a piece of candy wrapped in bright gold crinkly foil. "A sweet for a sweet," she said, placing the candy snugly into Spring-baby's palm. "Poor child. Everything is brief but God." She smiled again then turned to leave. A wheel squeaked with every rotation as she pushed the cart away and to the next room.

"Honey," Lorelei said after a moment during which the only sound was the squeaking wheel, "get dressed."

Spring-baby squeezed the gift as she might a baby's tender hand. "Okay, Mom," she said but didn't move until the squeak was heard no more.

Spring-baby sucked on the candy the short way to the funeral home, and when she walked with her mother past glinting cars and compassionate faces and into the tidy brick funeral home itself, the milky sweet taste of butterscotch lingered in a mouth now empty.

The foyer of the funeral home was a menagerie of subdued colors that smelled of stillness: plastic autumnal flowers on a small hardwood table polished deep brown; a settee, elegant

and antique but whose lace it wore like a mourning shroud; a
burgundy carpet, a stand for tissues, a lamp with a shade that
guarded well against the glare.

There were a couple of shut doors, but it was by one in
particular where the closest of kin stood.

"He looks like he's sleeping, just sleeping."

"I've been in already. I needed to be with him alone."

"Why can't he be like Lazarus? Oh, God help me."

"You ought to go in alone, Lorelei."

"Come here, Spring-baby. Let me tell you something."

It was her Uncle Kevin. His black tie swung away from his
slim body like a cloth pendulum as he leaned forward to stroke
her shoulder. "Listen to me, honey," he began in a voice as soft
as it was intense. "That's not your daddy in there. That's not
him. It's just a shell. Your daddy is in paradise with Jesus."

Spring-baby just nodded, but then she began to sniffle
anyway.

"Here, now" said a lady, handsome but for the affliction that
bowed and aged her beyond her years. "Hold Granny's hand."

It would have been well enough to say Death dwarfed
and belittled Spring-baby when she was finally led into the
viewing parlor were Death not to have the pallid countenance
at the time of one who would have certainly defended her.
There was her dad inside a casket ringed with bouquets. And
though her father looked somehow contrived in a suit and
though her father looked waxy, the imposter Spring-baby
sought was tragically absent.

She simply hadn't seen her father since she spied him from
the window, stepping off the back porch with a small tote in
hand and walking around the house and to the road with the
determination of a runner. It was as if she temporarily surfaced
from the depths of despair, so she crept up to the body and
kissed it welcome on the lips to the gasps and whispers of all
in attendance.

"Oh my, oh my!"

"Bless her little heart!"

But then coldness was on her own lips as she pulled away. And then coldness stayed with her as if it were her very own virus, doing the same thing to her system, shutting down her heart so that to continue on she would need a replacement. It was no good to be so young and cold and bereft of hope. Spring-baby stepped away from the corpse and braced herself against the early frost.

Suddenly, she felt her uncle's hand again on her shoulder.

"A shell. That's all. Jesus is savior."

At that time Spring-baby remembered Lazarus from Sunday school as if the memory were coaxed from her with each earnest stroke of her uncle's hand. There had been a felt Lazarus that walked out of a felt cave, and it had made her giggle. Jesus had been in the center of the display board with arms raised mightily. Her brother, Troy, had his thumb in his mouth right next to her where he had been told to behave.

Spring-baby nodded obediently without looking up at her uncle.

"Nothing more," he said. "He was a good man, a good brother. He was a good father to you."

But for the unrequited kiss, the viewing the next day was the same as that on the first day, yet on the day that followed, the cortege snaked its way in cars cleaned for the occasion to the church where they petitioned aloud, "Deliver me, O Lord, from eternal death in that awful day, when the heavens and the earth shall be shaken and Thou shalt come to judge the world by fire." Candles around the casket replaced the bouquets, and the priest at the front of the church had a robe that looked to Spring-baby like the one worn by the felt Jesus. She sat with her mother in the pew up front where candlelight glinted off of the casket's polished wood and golden handles.

At Saint Brigid Cemetery on the far edge of town,

mourners wreathed an empty hole and the box over it while an honor guard aimed and fired into the air three times sharply, ejecting spent cartridges over the manicured lawn after each boom. The discharges startled Spring-baby, even frightened her some, as she sat in a folding chair with her hand gripped by her mother, listening to the resonance and the weeping that spurted out of individuals from their murky, meditative wells.

She walked away as did everybody else before the casket was lowered, failing to avert her eyes from the displaced mound of clumpy red dirt spilling out from under the green tarpaulin placed as if to conceal a blemish. Her grandfather—a big-bellied, spectacled pygmy of a man whose prematurely white hair flamed from his balding scalp—clutched the flag folded into a triangle neither the mother nor the widow of the deceased could bear to carry. She got into the station wagon and waited, for there was to be a reception at the hall behind the Catholic Church. Someone nearby told her that she needed to get something into her stomach.

And so her plummet came as surely as rigor mortis. Spring-baby's eyes turned inward and stared at the abyss she didn't think possible. She was transfixed by it, imprinted by it; she was in communion with gloom. Her gaze never shifted, never gave her pardon, for the once-impossible abyss had ultimately become her last, sure love even though the ham sandwich filled her belly up and the maid with the German accent at the budget motel had never worked there to begin with.

II

The early morning fog cushioned the world against the coming day. Spring-baby was already up and sitting in the station wagon along with the suitcase she and her mother shared. Lorelei was in the dowdy lobby of the motel, trying to describe to the manager the maid who had given candy to her daughter.

"A stout woman, hefty. Sounded German, but then again I'm not good with accents."

"Ma'am," the manager replied, bellying up to the counter-top and looking at a loss. "This ain't a big operation. I run the front desk, mostly, and my wife and two daughters do up the rooms. Ain't one of them's German as far as I know." He finished with a shrug to which Lorelei responded with a disappointed grin.

Lorelei had wanted to say thank you or at least leave a sincere note. Each time she and Spring-baby had returned to the room to rest after a stint of public grieving they had invariably discovered a handful of candies in the middle of a made bed accompanied by an unassuming slip of paper on which was printed neatly, "Everything is brief but God." Even though anguish imprisoned them, keeping their eyes soppy and red, their emotional integrity ravaged and brittle, Lorelei and Spring-baby were both able to discern the kindness in the gesture. It had become a small thing to look forward to. Spring-baby had savored her butterscotch even after she had brushed her teeth, and Lorelei had found herself tucking away one or two into her purse for later.

By the time the station wagon turned into the wide blacktop driveway of a brick ranch house typical in size and style of many homes owned by the well-to-do of northern Kentucky, the sun had finally won its siege. The deep blue sky appeared heavy enough in its blueness to drop to the earth; the dew remaining on the newly clipped grass on either side of the driveway sparkled its swan song. A cement walkway from which protruded little white pebbles halted the driveway before the garage door then jutted past sprawling holly, creeping juniper, a decorative dogwood, and a small, neat hedge on its way to the front door. Spring-baby smelled the mint planted next to the house as she followed her mother indoors past a statuette of a black man holding a lantern searchingly.

Spring-baby's father was the son of the physician who delivered almost every baby in Vine Grove for the past twenty years, and who, in doing so, possessed an enviable mystique that happened to extend to his wife and three children, and when Spring-baby and Troy would visit, to them as well. In public, Spring-baby's grandfather was always Dr. Westbay, but in private, he was Fafa, the shrewd, oftentimes surly elder who admonished all his children to root hog or die, for that, he always said, could guarantee some measure of happiness in this world.

Yet as Spring-baby moped past a string of family portraits hung symmetrically on the beige wall that led into the dining room, the old man at the table was wearing a look that bespoke of another revelation—one as startling as it was evidently cruel. "Hi, Fafa," Spring-baby mumbled. The hardwood floor seemed to strain underneath her, though she certainly was not the biggest girl in her grade.

"Good morning," Fafa said blandly, for he had just woken up, and he was still trying to shake off the bitterness of having done so. He was sitting in his robe, pajamas, and moccasin-style slippers. "We got toast. Juice. Folks've been bringing over food for the last three days. Lorelei, coffee?"

Lorelei already had a blue speckled mug in her hand. "Yeah, a cup. Mom up?"

"She's still in the bathroom." He paused, lips beginning to quiver, a frown unable to bend low enough. Then he said, "Bathroom" and nothing more before he reached for his own cup of coffee, a ready gag.

Spring-baby pulled out a chair, trying not to let it scrape loudly against the floor, and sat far enough away from her grandfather to preserve his privacy. She was hungry, but she was too shy to ask for some juice let alone a piece of toast. She sat quietly, her hands flat underneath her thighs.

There was a wire basket on the kitchen countertop in which plastic eggs both brown and white were piled. Lorelei fondled them between sips of coffee.

"You went in alone, didn'tcha, Dad?"

"Went in alone where?"

"The viewing parlor. Where Mike was."

Fafa exhaled heavily through his nose as if he were trying to expel the memory of the sight of his dead son. "Yes," he replied.

Lorelei returned the plastic egg she had in her hand to the

basket. "I didn't." She put the mug on the countertop. "I was afraid. And now it's too late."

No one made a sound until Fafa finally said, "Mom rode with the hearse from Richmond. It was a ten-hour drive. About like from here to Pennsylvania."

"I know. That's what I heard. I'm his wife. I was his wife, though."

"Yes."

"I stayed in the foyer until most of the group went in."

"We buried my boy." Fafa slumped a little in his wire-backed chair. He didn't bother to push up the glasses that were resting visibly askew on the bridge of his thick, acne-scarred nose.

"I just couldn't," Lorelei continued. "Everybody said do it. You should do it. But I hadn't been alone with Mike since the day he ran home. We were so angry, so panicky. The things he said to me. The things I said to him."

From the narrow hallway adjoining the dining room, a door whimpered open then clicked shut. It took Granny a few moments to appear. Though only fifty-one, she used the wall as a guide, her shaky hand narrowly missing the bottoms of more frames holding the portraits of blood. Grief made her decrepit: her eyes, jaw, and the flesh around them seemed to want to drip to the floor.

"Come to see me before you go?"

"Yeah," said Spring-baby who until that point had never seen Granny in anything less than nice slacks and a blouse, for Dr. Westbay's wife sold real estate in the area, had built a name, and always looked presentable. Without make-up, she looked tired. The cotton nightgown she was wearing gave her the appearance of a little girl, and with that intimate correlation, Spring-baby grew a bit squeamish.

"You get'cha some breakfast? We got food on the counter."

"Can I have toast and juice?"

Granny plodded past Spring-baby and left a trail of cigarette odor. "Why sure, sure," she said, straining to sound pleasant. "I'll pull you down a plate, and your mom can fix it. How's
that?"

Spring-baby scooted out from the chair and accepted the
plate. Lorelei was untwisting the tie to the bread bag when she
said, "Mom, tell me about the ride; the one from Richmond.
Mike died at the VA hospital there because that's where the
specialist was, and you rode in the hearse all the way back
to Vine Grove." Lorelei inserted two pieces of bread into the
toaster, depressed the lever, grabbed the nearest napkin. She
pinched her nostrils with it but used the back of her hand to
intercept the trickling tears. "There's so much I still need to
say to him. Right there in front of him. You had ten hours,
and I'm his wife."

"I'm his mother," Granny interjected, her voice husky, pri-
mal—defensive even. "I made him a promise I wouldn't leave
him there or anywhere but here at home, so that's what I did.
I brought him back myself. I sat up front with the driver,
knowing I was keeping my word."

Lorelei waited, seemed to reassemble her feelings from
where they had been dismissed. "Yes, you're his mother. But me.
His wife." She gripped the countertop as she pleaded. "From
Richmond to Vine Grove. Tell me, please. I need to know what
you felt."

"No!"

"Honey," Fafa implored.

Spring-baby was able to reach the toast when it popped up.
The grape jelly was already out on the table.

"We called her day and night! We told her it was serious
and that she needed to come down!"

"I know. Please, dear."

"With two kids?" Lorelei exclaimed.

"They could've stayed with your mother!" Granny returned.

"He was their father!"

"You never wanted to believe how bad it was! Never!"

"I cleaned up his throw-up! I kept the kids away while he rested!"

"We tried to explain, but you wouldn't listen!"

Lorelei lifted her hands at a loss then let them fall to the countertop with a loud *whap*. "He left me once already, and now he left me again!" she cried. "I love him so much I can't stand him! He left me twice, and I still have something on my chest!"

Fafa was sobbing openly now, his body, diminutive next to most other men, convulsing as if trying to eject that which suffocated his soul. Spring-baby munched on her toast and sipped her juice, but there, too, was salt in each mouthful.

Granny clung weakly to the back of a chair. "He was too young," she moaned. "It's not supposed to be this way, a mother burying her child."

Lorelei rushed past Granny, past her daughter and Fafa to the front door, signaling her departure with a soft boom. It was as sudden as the flash removal of a Band-Aid. Spring-baby had finished her juice, and though she was still thirsty, she did not ask for more.

"It's not right," Granny said to herself, the air, to her dead son buried beneath the ground.

"Honey, sit down. Please."

Granny sat down in silence. The room remained silent. Spring-baby peeked up from her plate only hesitantly, afraid to disturb the sanctity of their sadness. Each grandparent looked through what was physically before them—candle-holders and candles, placemats, the wall with its many pictures—and seemed to be utterly arrested by memory: recent, unimaginable, immutable as time. A ceiling fan whirred. The morning sunbeams stretched through slits in the Venetian blinds and placed their golden brightness just before the darkest spot of them all.

Then the front door opened, but Lorelei did not step inside. She called, "Spring-baby! Come here!"

Spring-baby left her grandparents who seemed not to give Lorelei's call any heed.

"Mom?" Spring-baby said at the door.

Lorelei was standing outside. The suitcase was by her feet. "Mom needs time for Mom," she said hurriedly, glancing now and then above and beyond Spring-baby's head, the wounded smile never leaving her face. "It all happened so quickly. I didn't have time to think."

"Mom?" Spring-baby repeated, trepidation like an earthquake agitating the word.

"I need to take a little drive. That's all. Listen to Granny and Fafa."

She kissed her daughter on the forehead and ran: past the statuette, past the hedge, to the driver's side of the station wagon and the door that had been left open.

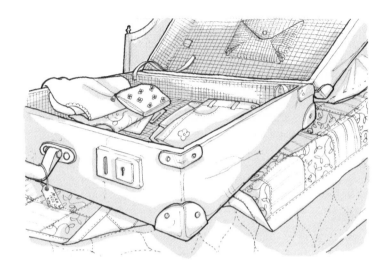

III

Fafa made phone calls to Pennsylvania throughout the morning but learned nothing about Lorelei's whereabouts. He called her mother and each one of her sisters but no one knew; they had no idea why she would do such a thing. And when he called them an hour or so later, Lorelei still hadn't checked in. It was a mystery to him and Granny both, but to Spring-baby, Lorelei's sudden departure was like having her life vest yanked from her as she bobbed and flailed in an open, hostile sea.

"I knew they married too young," Granny spat under her breath.

The truth was that Mike was only twenty and still posing for photos in his new Navy uniform when he met and betrothed the sister-in-law of a Marine he once attended

to while working as a corpsman at a hospital near Camp
LeJeune, North Carolina. Lorelei was there visiting, and Mike
had the weekend free. Within nine weeks, they were standing
at an altar in Lorelei's hometown in Pennsylvania, Mike
doughy but arresting in his dress blues, Lorelei as lovely in
a snow-white dress as any enamored eighteen year old would
be standing next to someone who wasn't from her hometown.
They both smiled as if immortal just before every click of
the camera.

Granny had never met Lorelei before making the trip up
to Pennsylvania with Dr. Westbay and the kids to witness the
wedding. She didn't know Lorelei from Eve, she had said, but
what she had known for certain was that Lorelei was the flesh
and blood result of an impulse. For better or worse, the fruit of
her womb would become of one body with another, untested
and strange. Granny had seen Lorelei stroll around her parent's
cottage home without shoes, even venturing outside onto the
wooden deck made out of two-by-fours and onto the lawn
that seemed to be nothing more than a tame outgrowth of the
woods around it. Lorelei had emerged as an unwary affront
toward Granny's worldview. Granny had to hide her disapprov-
ing grimaces more than once during their time there. There
were certain ways to do things: particular unwritten codes to
follow, appropriate behavior to adhere to. Lorelei had paid little
attention to convention, not out of spite but out of a common
upbringing. All of this, Granny had soon been able to discern
in her abrupt daughter-in-law; this girl, though pleasant, might
as well have been from a different country. So while Fafa was
on the phone off and on during the morning, the shock of
Lorelei's flight quickly waned for Granny, settling instead into
an irked wisdom.

"Just two outfits. And one pair of shorts is practically
threadbare," Granny said out loud, not really expecting to
find anything different. She was poking through the suitcase

Spring-baby all but dragged indoors, and she was thinking with her hands, trying to respond to what Lorelei had done. She clamped the suitcase shut with an exasperated sigh. "I suppose your mother will call us sometime," she said to Spring-baby who stood next to her, believing that the miniscule space she occupied beneath her feet was too much for Granny to tolerate.

This wasn't the case, of course, but Spring-baby understood her place in the universe as poor relations understand theirs: grateful but with spare self-esteem. She was used to flapping, unglued heels on her shoes and to sharing cans of pop and toothbrushes with her brother. It was a way of self-reflection she inherited from her mother who didn't grow up with money or spotlights or trumpets and who never had a bed of her own, having first shared a bed with her sisters, and then a bed with her husband. The first night Lorelei ever slept alone, in fact, was when Mike left to die—the mattress as vast and lonely as a broken heart. When she'd periodically wake, she'd pace about, mostly, eclipsing the line of light beneath Spring-baby and Troy's bedroom door with every pass. That same night, Spring-baby slept fitfully in her very own bed, too, intently aware of her mother's distress and unable to understand why guilt mingled with sadness as she lay on the single mattress she was told cost eighty dollars and could only be purchased on lay-away.

"No rhyme or reason," Granny uttered fraily, shaking her head and eyeing her son's daughter through grief-swollen lids. "Of all the rotten times."

They were left with nothing and everything to assume, save only that Lorelei's hiatus would more than likely last at least a night, given that she had left Spring-baby with the suitcase after having rifled through it to extract her own few clothes, toothbrush, and toothpaste. Spring-baby was given her Aunt Marissa's old bedroom: a lavender-walled sanctuary for the things of a well-kept girl. A cedar chest on which was

assembled a pretty choir of dolls sat at the foot of a bed
with a comforter so generous, it looked like risen dough. There
was a dresser in one corner of a quality Spring-baby couldn't
even imagine her parents owning, and next to it was a vanity—
brushes and barrettes placed at orderly, showy angles on its
dustless surface in front of a tall, three-paneled mirror. Too,
there were framed prints depicting soft pastoral scenes: butterflies on flowers, birds aloft and singing. And the windows
had billowy, white curtains—like frosting on a store-bought
cake. The carpets even smelled faintly new, and Spring-baby
found herself wanting to remove her shoes before she walked
in entirely.

The day eventually happened like evaporation happens and
with similar effect. As the clock ticked audibly, each grandparent sat cloistered in separate rooms in order to stare blankly
at separate pains, and all Spring-baby's childish hope for her
mother's quick return slowly flaked away into an infinite atmo-
sphere. She ate when Granny temporarily emerged to make
her a lunch of a peanut butter and jelly sandwich and some
potato chips. She drifted throughout the house, looking at
family pictures and, when she found them, the books with
mildly entertaining medical diagrams on her Fafa's many and
randomly-placed bookshelves. She sat alone in maturely deco-
rated rooms, kicking her feet listlessly. Though a television set
tempted her from where it was ensconced in a dark corner of
the living room, it ultimately remained off because Spring-baby
did not want to presume upon her grandparents by creating
any sound.

To Spring-baby's recollection, never had this house been
awash in such staggering bleakness. The thing her grandparents
had contracted others to build years ago had become a cher-
ished cocoon to those who called it home, never mind going to
school, being married off, or being transferred from one Navy
base to another until being squarely deposited by fate in a

small town in northern Appalachia. Home, to her dad, was a
feeling as much as it was a place, and when he took his wife
and kids there to be with those who knew him as brother and
son, nephew and grandchild, it was a reunion of a fractured
soul. The thing that was a house was renewed in its purpose
as a home.

The virus only heightened her dad's need to sleep and wake
in a place as familiar to him as his own name. The sicker he
got, the more Pennsylvania became obscenely foreign to him
and the stronger his home in Kentucky pulsed its beckon. Even
the years he had already won were whittled away as death
encroached, leaving him a boy in a man's failing body who
would have called a do-over if it were at all possible. There
grew to be more sojourns to Kentucky and extra days spent
reminiscing, forgetting, wishing disbelief. They were pathetic
yo-yo flights for her father—from Pennsylvania, down and
back up—yet for Spring-baby they were simply times when
the air was sweeter and bedtimes were forgotten and everybody
told her how big she was getting as if they were astronomers all
charting the path of a single star.

With her dad laid to rest, the house through which she
now drifted had become a thing again: a soulless chamber
made of brick and wood. It was a testament to the avarice
of death to take more than just the deceased. The house was
its own museum, haunted as much by the joy that once was
as by the happy, framed faces peering outward behind glass
encasements pressed to their noses.

Spring-baby walked the rooms until she was flung outside
by the force of boredom and the weariness of melancholy.

Her grandparents' ranch house was built into a slope that
fed, at the bottom, into a fenced-in pasture belonging to a
neighbor whose dirty white house sat on the next rise at the
end of an unpaved lane amidst a copse of pines. A barn,
its exterior sooty with age, occupied the lower corner of the

pasture nearest the property line, and on her grandparents' side of the fence was a robust willow tree with limbs that tickled the roof of the barn with every puff of wind. There, in one of the willow's hulky crooks, Spring-baby would sometimes sit during her dad's visits, content in being elevated, often lazily tossing peeled-away pieces of bark or pocketed stones onto the roof of the barn or wherever she so desired.

She crammed her shorts pockets with stones taken from beside the road in front of her grandparents' house and then took her time traipsing to the willow tree out back. She walked along the shady side of the house to avoid having to squint against the sun that was, even then in the late afternoon, beaming hard and bright, and she decapitated the occasional dandelion along the way. Then the sporadic blast of a train's horn, followed by the train itself rumbling just beyond another distant neighbor's property, caught Spring-baby's attention, stopping her in the sun-baked yard and leaving her to wonder what it would be like to ride away in one of the train's lumbering cars. But the train eventually passed, so Spring-baby jogged the rest of the way to the willow tree because that was the next best thing to do.

The trunk was squat enough for Spring-baby to claw and muscle her way up using protruding knots and young branches. Her spot was the crook above the first split in the aged tree: a perch like a saddle comfortably high above the ground and sheltered by slender, drooping, living twigs. There, she remained mounted and alone, casting stones at random targets as if she were at a fairground dime toss.

First it was a grayish, weathered fence post that appeared to be just as much held up by the barbed wire it was supposed to keep taut. Then it was a certain vertical plank on the side of the barn. Every time she'd hit her target, she'd move on to find another. It took a few stones to strike the fence post, but she got lucky with the plank. The stone connected with a

sharp knock then fell into the tall spray of weeds that hemmed
the base of the barn as far as the cross-paneled door, which,
as Spring-baby spied it, was latched to a rusty hook, leaving
the entrance itself gaping, dark, and not a little foreboding.
Spring-baby fixed on the entrance—no doubt for the curiosity
it piqued—and wondered what kind of animal packed the soil
there tight and flat, whatever could have made the few earthen
tributaries that meandered from the entrance until disappear-
ing into the uneven field. She had not been aware of an animal
in her lifetime ever grazing in the pasture, ever living in the
barn—had neither seen one or heard the adults speak of one
being introduced. Yet nothing stepped forth, and Spring-baby
saw only a vacant field and a barn entrance wide enough to
swallow her, empty enough to mock her. The entrance had
become a yawning, inviting hole—a black ugly expanse into
which she could hurl the whole uncompromising world. So in
her throwing hand she rolled a stone, testing it for its shape,
and when she found the best grip, she pulled back angrily and
took careful aim.

The donkey clopped out of the barn and into view and
stood sleepily and unassumingly still, perhaps acclimating to
the sunrays that now made his light-gray coat appear to
thaw and shimmer. There was nothing at all unique about
this animal: dark, glossy eyes protruding from a shaggy face,
ears that projected determinably from a lolling head, a white
muzzle, a stupid tail, a bristly, unkempt mane. He was just a
donkey, placid and typical, standing there as unwarily as any
sacrifice.

Spring-baby let fly the stone, striking the donkey in the
flank with a dull, dusty thud. The donkey winced, grunted—
reared away from the direction of the impact.

Being mean for Spring-baby felt good in the worst possible
way because, in the end, she remained a little girl in a big tree
who just wanted something in this world to hate.

If it could have even been called a triumph, it was short-lived, for a slouchy man wearing a ragged T-shirt and blue jeans that hung from a fleshless backside and bunched at the ankles tore around the corner of the barn with a warding finger. "Hey, there! Girl in the tree! Why you throw a rock?"

He stopped just outside of the shade of the tree limb on which Spring-baby sat, one hand akimbo and the other still raised. "I seen you do it!" he yelled. He appeared to be more hurt than angry. His nostrils tightened on his beak nose; consternation cinched his bushy eyebrows. Spring-baby thought she even saw his frown twitch as if ready to fold under the weight of his dismay. He was young and balding and would not have been intimidating had he not caught her being honest.

"I didn't mean it," she offered weakly.

"Fibber! You din't see me, but I seen you!"

"I'm sorry."

She had by then maneuvered herself off from her special crook and began to climb back down to the first split in the tree from where, she was sure, she could get away in a hurry.

"How would you like it if somebody throw a rock at you? Prob'ly hurt, huh?"

"I won't do it again," she said, working her way down impatiently and feeling the unrelenting sting of his eyes on her.

When she finally slid and scraped her way to a place where she could stand erect and ready, the man gestured her toward him.

"Come here, come here," he said.

Spring-baby got down from the willow tree completely.

The stranger called her over again, both hands lowered now but still frowning and expecting. But she was more ashamed than willing, and besides, she had thrown her last stone.

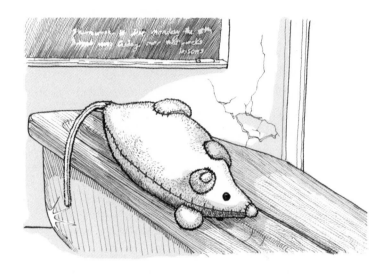

IV

S pring-baby had only just finished the sixth grade where she learned about Narnia and Terabithia and the location of Venezuela, and where she begrudgingly multiplied and divided fractions on low-grade, lined sheets of paper. But what she did not learn was how to identify shame for what it was, so instead, she thought of the girl—a useful surrogate for the donkey and the stone—who carried a stench and who wore the same two bargain-store dresses, each one on alternating days as if no one noticed.

For the class Christmas party, Spring-baby had drawn her name, which meant that they were to exchange presents. Spring-baby had given her a stuffed mouse—pink-eared and huggable—and she had received in return a deck of Flintstone playing cards, but Ms. Friel, the teacher, didn't think the trade equitable.

"Is this all you got Spring-baby?" Ms. Friel said to the girl, holding the deck of cards as one would hold soiled underwear.

"Yes," the girl answered, one thin arm around the mouse's neck.

"This is unacceptable. You should be ashamed of yourself." She flung the deck of cards onto the girl's small desk then snatched the mouse just as curtly. "You don't deserve this toy. I'm giving it back to Spring-baby. And you can just keep these cards and think about what you've done."

The girl cried for the rest of the afternoon while Spring-baby looked on with the stuffed mouse sitting untouched and unwanted on her desk. Never a word was shared between them: the girl because she could finally smell herself, and Spring-baby because she, in fact, had once called the girl scummy to her face and because she had wrinkled her nose for all the class to see when she drew the girl's name from the red Santa hat.

Spring-baby had ended up leaving the stuffed mouse on the desk, though as she sat on the cement stoop where her mother had said her hasty goodbye, she wished painfully that she had done so much more and said so much less. She was still feeling sorry for herself when Fafa pulled open the door and stuck out his unhappy head.

"Spring-baby."

"Yeah."

"Hungry? We haven't heard from your mother."

"Okay."

"Come on inside. It's getting dark."

They ate potato salad from flimsy paper plates; they bit into hamburger buns between which were ham and turkey slices and Swiss cheese slathered with mustard.

No one spoke until Spring-baby said, "I saw the donkey out back. Did you know there was a donkey?"

Fafa finished swallowing. "He moseys around. I've seen him, but I think he's new."

"Every so often they got some animal wandering around that field," said Granny, resting her fork on her plate.

"I've never seen him before," Spring-baby continued. "There was a man down there, too, that I've never seen before either."

Fafa slurped his coffee, and the slurp was louder for how it pervaded the resilient shush. "You must be talking about Chirp Vanhoosen," he said, returning his mug to the table. "He works around the barn. He still lives alone up in that white house—been alone since his mother died. Probably never will move out. Why? He say something about your dad?"

"No," replied Spring-baby.

"Mike is a few years older that him, but he'd pal around with him every so often. Chirp's what you call mentally retarded. Not severe, though."

"He is?"

"He's just slow," Granny said. "Mike would toss the ball with him."

"I didn't know Dad was nice to him."

"Your dad was a nice guy, a nice guy," Fafa said in earnest. He took a long sip of coffee.

Granny pushed herself away from the table, but she did not rise. She remained transfixed as if watching the last bubbles leave her drowning body. Then she said, "At a time like this."

"I know, honey."

"I love you so much," she said to Spring-baby, a tear wasting away as it traveled down her face.

"I love you too, Granny."

She turned slowly to her husband who, like her, had aged ten years in a week's time. "What did she want me to say? I gave him birth. I was with him before they wheeled him into the operation room. My boy, my boy. The ride back from Richmond was for me and him only."

"You did what Mike asked," Fafa said reassuringly.

Granny lifted her gaze from her husband then let it slowly descend onto her granddaughter. "I'm fifty-one years old, Spring-baby. Did you know that about your granny?"

Spring-baby did not.

"You made me a grandmother. How about that?" She smiled a little. "I had just turned thirty-nine. But your dad made me a mother. I was a kid, really. Eighteen. We were in San Diego, and Fafa was in the Navy and out on a ship somewhere in the Pacific. Your dad always wanted to be like your grandfather."

A moment passed during which not a word was uttered. No one could really escape, so no one moved, no one tried. Instead, Granny appeared to be trying to reconfigure the shards she was left with. She looked at her granddaughter's face, pleaded with the sleepy, hazel eyes, the rounded chin, the unapologetic nose—all like her father's. Another tear trickled unannounced down Granny's cheek.

"An arm's length," she continued. "Did you know that a newborn baby can only see as far away as the distance of his mother's arm? The whole world is a blur. For a time, I was all your daddy knew. I was the face he understood best."

"I was on a hospital ship for close to nine months," Fafa interjected gently. "I was a corpsman like your dad. Granny used to send me pictures of your dad, and she kept pictures of me for him to look at to learn who I was."

Granny let him finish, then added, "He was my only child for six years before Kevin came then Marissa after that. He wasn't perfect. No. He used to frustrate me to no end, it seemed. So impulsive. So . . ." She kept the last thought to herself and sat with it before she went on. "But he was my son before he was anybody's husband and even before he was your daddy. How can a mother share what that means? Why would a mother want to?" At that, she pushed herself up from her seat but did not step away just yet. "The driver—he's a good friend of the family—never said one word to me the whole way back from Virginia." This was how she concluded because she abruptly turned and walked back down the hallway and into her bedroom. The *ka-click* was pronounced as she closed the door behind her.

"Roy Holmberg," Fafa said. "He's a real nice guy. We've known him for years." Then he, too, staggered upward from his chair and joined his wife in the bedroom.

Perhaps Spring-baby had been introduced to Roy Holmberg as Dr. Westbay's granddaughter, but she had no recollection of such an encounter. There was simply no room for the memory. Instead, she extended her arm and stretched out her hand and studied the length to the tips of her fingers. "Yabba dabba doo," she mouthed. Then she laid her arm on the table.

V

When Spring-baby went to bed, there was no phone call from her mother, and when she awoke the next day, there was none either. Immediately after she ate toast, she walked down to the pasture, her feet mopping up the morning dew along the way.

Chirp Vanhoosen was carrying a bucket into the barn, the water inside the bucket sloshing to and fro with each teetering step. He stopped when he saw her approaching.

"I'm sorry about the rock," she blurted. She had walked right up to the barbed wire fence. Her eyes were a few inches above the uppermost wire. "I didn't mean to hurt your donkey."

He set down the bucket, turned to face her directly. "My donkey," he started, but it was no use. First, the laugh came airily, but then it gained deeper bass notes as the very idea became clearer to him. "Amen just poof!" He threw up his hands, acted surprised. "I find him walking around the pasture eating grass. I know his name 'cause he tell me it."

"What's his name?" Spring-baby heard herself ask. The donkey was nowhere to be seen.

"Amen," replied Chirp Vanhoosen.

"Like in church?"

Chirp Vanhoosen shrugged his shoulders, an idiotic grin never leaving his stubbly face.

"Do you think I hurt him?" Spring-baby asked. "Can I see him? I don't see him in the field."

"He ain't in the field. He's in the barn. He's eating 'cause I give him food like I do every morning." There was a coyness about his manner—the way he sucked in his lips as if they would betray his secret, the way his eyes seemed to crouch. He chuckled. "You prob'ly give him a start, maybe, but as far as hurt him—naw. You should know what I know."

"What's that?"

"I know Amen walk away from a lot more than a little girl and a rock." He carefully wiped his calloused hands on his thighs, leaned in, finally croaked mysteriously, "He's older than death."

Spring-baby might have been unsettled by this unusual proclamation had the half-wit standing in front of her not had the disarming presence of a boy Troy's age. Because he was not angry like he had been the day before, he was not in the least bit imposing, even though he was a grownup. His droopy body, to Spring-baby, remained nothing more than a veneer for someone with whom she could be direct, so she said, "My name's Spring-baby. I know you're Chirp Vanhoosen. My dad and you played together, but he's dead."

She was amused by how he imagined the donkey poofing into existence, talking to him so matter-of-factly. Still, Chirp

Vanhoosen sounded about as stupid as Raymond Barheit in her grade who wet himself in front of everybody just last year and who had to go to a special class in the afternoon.

Chirp Vanhoosen continued: "I know your dad's way away."

"He was a good man."

"Yep," he nodded. "But you see, Amen, why, he tell me this one time how when he was borned, there was no way away, not even the notion." Chirp Vanhoosen bunched up his mouth and nodded some more but slowly, assuredly.

"Everything is brief but God," remembered Spring-baby aloud.

"I know that," replied Chirp Vanhoosen. "My mommy tell me that, but she gone way away too." Then he added, "She like it when Mike throw the ball to me."

"I saw the dirt they threw on him—on his casket, I mean."

Chirp Vanhoosen finally stepped closer to Spring-baby, rested one arm on a post. He was close enough for Spring-baby to smell his damp sweat, but "scummy" never crossed her mind.

He said, "That Amen, he tells me funny things but not all what makes you laugh."

"I know my mommy and daddy, but Amen, he never know his. He say he just find himself walking around and eating grass and enjoying the sunshine 'cause it sunshined all the time. He live in a place with a lot of grass and a lot of trees and streams and birds and other animals, even the ones that would eat him nowadays. But not back then. When he was tired, he sleept, and when he wasn't, he was up and about. Nothing or anybody try to hurt him or throw rocks at him. He like that place, it was nice, and the grass was good, too. Amen din't even need someone like me to give him water. He din't drink his water from a basin at all.

"You know Adam, right, and Eve from turch?"

"You mean church?" Spring-baby shrugged. "I go some-times."

"Yes, I go to turch. I learn about Adam and Eve, too, but let me tell you something you prob'ly won't believe: Amen, he meet them—'cause he's that old. That old. I tell you, and you need to believe me."

Eve was a rib. She was Adam's best friend. Adam, he listen to his daddy 'cause he knew him, not like Amen, and Eve did, too, and they were naked and happy 'cause I guess it din't get cold there.

You 'member I said there was no death then 'cause that's what Amen, he tell me?

There was no graveyards like the one my mommy's in, which is Saint Brigid.

Amen, he had nothing to do with it, but a snake fib to that Eve, and she turn around and got Adam to eat, too, 'cause they weren't supposed to eat from that tree, and there it was, death, and no more good grass and sunshine all day long.

And you know what else, but animals got kilt and Adam take the fur and wear it, and there was blood on the ground. It was the first blood on the ground. Eve wore skins, too. Amen, he hide 'cause he din't know what he seen was death. He said Adam and Eve's faces was ugly, too. The animals scream. It was cold on the outside of the place 'cause that's where they had to go. Amen, he had to go, too, and he din't even try the fruit.

Inside the place, Adam was real nice to Amen, but on the outside, he was stern and yelling. He got mean, and animals try to hurt him, too, you know, eat him up.

Enough was enough, say Amen, so he point himself west and start to walk back to where he din't have to wait for green grass to grow 'cause it was always there, and off he run until he got tired. Then he just walk, but he din't stop even when it got dark. Well, it got cold and the stars were only halfways out and he was thirsty. And just then Amen hear'd a noise that make his spine grow colder and he pick up the pace. But that din't do no good 'cause what it was was a lion: a big one, growling, with claws like a garden rake. I would be scared, and I bet you would, too. So Amen turn, and the lion come up growling, and Amen figgers no more green grass for me. He rears up like donkeys do, you know, his hooves boxing the air to frighten the lion away. But the lion show him his teeth. It would never have showed him his teeth before, but Amen, he was too scared to be sad. He box the air some more, but it was Adam that scream onto the scene with rocks and big sticks. I guess the lion din't want to bother Amen no more 'cause he run away. But you couldn't see where 'cause the moon was only halfways out, too, and it was prob'ly Adam's daddy anyways that made the lion run, really.

When Adam catch his breath, he tie Amen with a rope and tell him, "Donkey, I'm not through with you!" Just like that then he drag him back and tie him up, which was the first time Amen ever been tie up.

Adam give Amen water when they got back, but Amen couldn't stop thinking how in the place where it sunshined a lot nobody show him their teeth and nobody tie him up with a rope or nothing like that. And now he was tie up next to Adam and Eve where it was cold and dark. It make him cry but not like we do 'cause he's a donkey, but it's almost the same.

The final thought left him satisfied and silent. He stood there for a moment, thinking, perhaps merely wondering. Eventually

he sighed. Spring-baby hadn't offered much of anything in the
way of a response to his story about Amen's beginnings.

She remained planted, fingers absently plucking the uppermost length of barbed wire. When Chirp Vanhoosen stooped
to pick up the buckets, though, she finally said, "He said all
that? Donkeys don't really talk. Not really."

All Chirp Vanhoosen did was pick up the two buckets and
start to walk away.

"Hey!" Spring-baby called. "Donkeys don't really talk!"

But Chirp Vanhoosen didn't turn around. He just disappeared into the barn, mumbling something about death and
talking donkeys and what people choose to believe.

Soon, Spring-baby could hear water being dumped, one
bucketful after the other. Then there was nothing. She didn't
move. She remained and remembered that her dad's lips were
cold, lifeless. What did the retard know about that?, she thought.
Didn't he know that he had been talking to death itself?

Despair, sadness—these things she was sure of. Not immutable bliss, not leather and Old Spice, and certainly not a
donkey who could recall the time before death had come into
the world. Hers was a faith in undeserved loss—a faith in
what does happen, not in what should. Spring-baby knew what
mentally retarded meant even if Fafa hadn't told her. And only
a retard would suggest there had once been a place without
graveyards.

Still, she lingered, and neither man nor donkey emerged
from the barn. Spring-baby pulled down the barbed wire until
it was stretched taut. But when she realized what she was
waiting for, she turned abruptly and started back up to the
house. As she walked, she attempted to smother her curiosity,
but her mind, nevertheless, kept drifting back to the inside of
the barn, the man, the donkey, the stall door between them.
Even so, she walked without looking back. She walked and
wept fiercely.

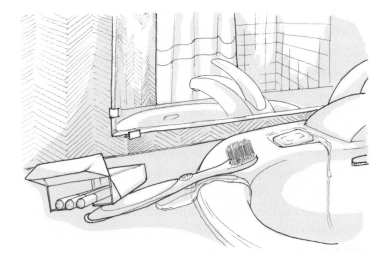

VI

Everybody knew Granny was a smoker. Her habit was to disappear into the bathroom, and with canned air freshener as her octopus ink, spritz the area immediately outside the bathroom to conceal any smell that might seep out. Everybody ignored her politely. More than likely, only Fafa knew exactly in what manner she'd smoke, whether she'd slump cross-legged on the toilet in a restful daze or whether she'd lean against the wall like a high-schooler taking a respite from propriety. The real secret was that everybody knew hers, so if there was any mystery about her sojourns, it would be the brand of cigarettes she smoked. Only Fafa had a guess, and that he kept to himself.

Spring-baby learned early to be mum. She had heeded the surreptitious shushes of her mother or her father so well that she imagined herself shushing her little brother when his nose would wrinkle at the smell like hers once had. Before her dad died, she was even beginning to enjoy the power of holding the secret as if its possession gave her more clout. Indeed, she would occasionally share with an adult a darting look of mutual knowledge, and for those times, she looked forward to Granny's smoke breaks very much. Silence was a good thing. Those who kept it, kept the peace by keeping each other—this community of the happy dumb—and Spring-baby was well pleased with herself that she could hold her tongue like a big girl.

Chirp Vanhoosen should know better even though he probably once had to go to a special class in the afternoon. There were certain unmentionables never to be broached or otherwise disturbed. Dad's vigils. Granny's cigarettes. The memory of her dad's cold, dead lips on her own lips was very intimate, very real, and no story could dilute that memory— give it perspective, render it anonymous.

It was as if Chirp Vanhoosen had kicked down the bathroom door and held up a pack of Virginia Slims for all the world to see, trivializing Granny's private moment, Spring-baby's grief.

She was sitting with these thoughts at the kitchen table when Granny walked out of the bathroom and said, "Mamau and Aunt Boo will be over in a bit. You like fried chicken, don't you? They're bringing over a bucket for lunch."

Mamau was Granny's mother, and Mamau and Aunt Boo were identical twins. They lived in separate residences just across town in order to pretend autonomy, though Granny increasingly ran groceries and medication over to them both at least twice a week. Mamau and Aunt Boo were kindly vestiges of days when women didn't wear blue jeans or sit with their knees apart. They each wore horn-rim glasses, purchased some twenty years ago, and were dressed always as if going to church: blouses tucked into mono-colored skirts pulled high on the waist, length to the shins, and matching shoes. Both called their husbands Mister when their husbands were still around to be called anything but dead. Both were incurable doters, sticking dollar bills into the birthday cards they always sent. Everything about the two was practically the same but for their very different dispositions, for while Aunt Boo's glass was always half full, Mamau's glass was perpetually half empty, the water probably not good for drinking anyway.

"Mercy, mercy, mercy," Mamau drawled after patting the corners of her mouth with a napkin. "Girl's probably who-knows-where without a thought of looking back to see who's standing in the dust."

"I don't know why she did it," said Granny.

"It starts in the home," Mamau continued. "You seen her run around without no shoes. Lord'a mercy."

"It's not right of her."

"Nothing in this world's right. Only when we meet our Maker does it all come out even. She ain't called, has she?"

"No. And as far as I know not anybody else."

"Lord'a mercy," Mamau lamented again.

"I could have changed Lorelei's diapers," Aunt Boo chimed in. She was sitting next to her sister, pleasantly finishing a chicken breast. "And so could have you," she added, addressing Granny. "She'll call or turn up soon most likely. Ain't nothing to fret over. And besides, Lorelei being gone gives Spring-baby more time to spend with her Aunt Boo." She smiled brightly and said, "Isn't that right, honey? You know Aunt Boo would do anything for you. I mean it. You know I mean it."

Spring-baby showed that she knew Aunt Boo meant it by returning the smile. She was truly fond of Aunt Boo, called so because Spring-baby's dad had once been unable to pronounce Flossie.

"I just love you, love you, love you."

"Don't you forget it that your Mamau loves you, too," Mamau said, not to be outdone.

"I know Mamau," said Spring-baby.

"And I love that brother of yours, too. Poor, poor baby."

Fafa lifted up his head from a small pile of chicken bones and said, "It was something about not going into the viewing parlor, that's what I gather. Who knows anything anymore."

"I know what's right and what isn't," said Granny, stirred out of her thoughts. "Barefoot. Barefoot in the lawn."

Mamau sniffled. "Impulsive, but I loved him so."

"All of us did," joined Aunt Boo. She turned to Spring-baby and said, "Your daddy loved you so much."

"Where did Mom go?" asked Spring-baby. "I didn't do anything. It's not my fault."

"It's not your fault is right," echoed Aunt Boo. "But sometimes bad luck just comes even when you're doing the best you can. Your mother just has to get her bearings is all." She stretched over and patted Spring-baby's leg.

"You listen to your Aunt Boo, now, and you listen to me." Mamau pulled herself more erect and pursed her lips no nonsense, leaned in, locked eyes. "It wasn't your fault no how. Your mom's just 'different people'."

"Where'd she go?"

"Away. That's all we know."

"Why couldn't I go?"

Fafa sighed.

"You know your Aunt Boo used to help make shoes," Aunt Boo said. "In Louisville, I did, for twenty years till I stopped and worked at a nursery."

"I did, too." Mamau said. "Tough work right alongside her except I wasn't in the nursery because I was married to Papau then."

Spring-baby could barely remember the quiet old gentleman who once drove Mamau to the house for visits.

"You finished with your plate?" Granny asked Spring-baby before taking it anyway. She put it on the countertop, headed for the bathroom.

"I loved those little ones," Aunt Boo reminisced.

"I've never seen my mom cry before. She cried on the phone when Fafa called and Gramma was there, and she shook the bed so I couldn't sleep."

Mamau said sadly, "I haven't been able to sleep a wink." Then her gaze drifted away and fell frozen upon the floor.

Fafa grunted but just barely. He hadn't slept well either, the skin beneath his eyes like ashen mudslides down his cheeks.

The ceiling fan whirred.

"I cried a lot, too," Spring-baby said.

"The phone," Fafa murmured. "I got to use the phone. There's no sense in waiting for a call that probably won't come anytime soon. Dr. Biord's covering for me, but I suspect he's got questions about this one patient of mine who comes in just about every week with something or another the matter. There's a way to handle him." At that, he got up and walked tiredly over to the phone, dialed, waited, turned away to talk when Dr. Biord presumably answered.

"You cry all you want to," Aunt Boo said, perking up a bit, rippling the still pool the room had become. "I do and will do later. Crying's good. There's no shame to be had."

"My mom cried like I did one time when I wrecked on my bike coming down Pool Hill. I slid in the gravel and bled a lot. I cried all the way home and even when Dad cleaned me up."

"I bet," said Aunt Boo. "I bet it hurt something awful." She looked downward, her gaze matching Mamau's for a moment, but then she looked back up as if she had only looked down to retrieve a thought. "Did you know your Aunt Boo had a son?"

Spring-baby did not. Spring-baby had never wondered why

Aunt Boo did not have any children.

"His name was Wayne, but we called him Butchie. When he was old enough to walk, he walked out into the road when I wasn't looking and got hit and killed. I saw the whole thing: him toddling along, him stepping off the curb. The car was flat black. The woman driver said she didn't see him, and I believed her, but what are words, what are words when…" She stopped, bit the lip that was starting to quake. "Oh Lordy, Lordy, mercy me. I cried borrowed tears. Yes, ma'am."

"That's sad," Spring-baby said.

"That's all there was for me anymore," Aunt Boo said after a moment. "Every waking minute, every asleep one, too. All there was for me was an ache as big as water is wet. There just couldn't be any other way." Aunt Boo smoothed out her skirt and rested her hands on her knees.

Mamau continued to stare through the world, at once consumed and oblivious though she only sat a few feet away.

Spring-baby thought. Then she said, "Mine is as big as water is wet, too. Dad died on the first day of summer vacation, but I didn't think of that until now."

"Oh, Spring-baby," Aunt Boo replied gently. "I'm older than what you can count on both hands and both feet. I came to know one way, but I tell you the truth, I eventually came to know another."

"What's that? What's another?"

"Growing old has a way of shedding light here and turning out the lights elsewhere. I cried for my baby years upon years until I woke up and realized I had been leaking tears over a lie."

"A lie?"

"Crying's good, I said. It's good, no shame."

"But why a lie?"

"'Cause all that time, here I've been told dying makes you dead." Aunt Boo grinned confidently. It was a grin that loved, entreated.

Spring-baby stared blankly.

"You're twelve years old," Aunt Boo continued matter-of-factly.

"Yes."

"I was a girl, too, once." Her grin slowly dissolved into something mellower. "It took me a lifetime to realize that there's a lot of what if left in me, never mind it's all under these wrinkles you see here now. I know the day starts with the sunrise. I used to think it started with the sunset."

Just then, Spring-baby remembered the dew on her feet.

"I'm tired," Mamau said, coming unthawed. "Feels like later. Stomach full of chicken about put me to sleep."

Aunt Boo looked at her sister. "That was yummy, wasn't it?"

"A mite greasy for me."

Fafa hung up the phone about the same time Granny emerged from the bathroom.

Mamau said to anyone who would listen, "I suspect I should go back home and lay this body down for a while."

So she did, and she took Aunt Boo with her, but not before she told Spring-baby, bless her heart, how much of a good daddy Mike had been.

VII

Spring-baby was small enough to slip between the lowest and middle wires without getting barbed or too dirty. On the pasture side of the fence, she surveyed the land for the retard and the donkey but spied neither. Above, darkly laden cumuli converged, stacked one on top of the other, slowed, prepared.

Back at the house, Granny continued to oscillate between bathroom and bedroom. Fafa had eventually fled to the office. There was still no phone call, and even the expectation of one had grown as faint as a star discovered at dawn.

Overhead, the clouds spoke their throaty intent. Spring-baby stopped at the open entrance and called out.

There was no response. The beaten path leading into the barn emptied into a mute, lightless place—the things contained therein, shadowy forms that, together, pulsed lethargically compared to the things without. Pine straw sprinkled the sullen ground. A shovel, its business end wide enough to scoop up manure, leaned against an aged post. To the side, there was an empty wheelbarrow that appeared as if it might have been painted yellow, and suspended from a hook just above it was a harness and a small coil of rope. For the most part, the short row between the stalls was clear. A hoe was propped next to a stall door further in, and at the far end of the row was a mass of something covered in tarpaulin. Supervising it all was a wooden beam on which was painted, "No smokin'."

Spring-baby was acclimating to the cooped, heavy barn air when she heard from behind, "Toldja so."

She turned around only slightly startled because she had imagined she'd see Chirp Vanhoosen anyway. "I want to see Amen. I want to say something to him."

"He ain't here."

"Where is he?"

"Don't know. I turn my back on him, and when I turn back around he was gone. He does that, so I ain't worried. He poofs. He's a poofing donkey."

"He'll be back?"

"Don't see why not. He come back every other time."

"When? When will that be?"

"Don't know, but if you look and wait it'll be longer."

Spring-baby looked and waited nevertheless. She looked into the barn. "Which one is his?"

"Which one what?"

"Stall. I know that donkeys and horses stay in stalls at night."

Chirp Vanhoosen sidled up to Spring-baby, pointed a finger to nowhere in particular. "This one, that one. It all depends. He's whatcha call antsy."

"Antsy?"

"He ain't even here, is he? He's busy, that's what he tell me."

Spring-baby glanced down at her girl feet and walked her glance up to her girl legs, hands, and arms. She paused only briefly on the glands that had just recently begun to grow. "What else has he told you?" she said.

Chirp Vanhoosen hiked up his sagging jeans and strode to a place just inside the barn where he could lean like the tools there. "Spring-baby," he began. It was the first time he used her name. "I wouldn't believe it myself if it weren't coming from a donkey what talks."

"That harness just hangs there on the post 'cause I don't use it. I ain't mean. Or the rope either: to tie Amen up and drag him around. Amen got drug around a lot. From one person to the next he got hit and drug, but not me. I feed him every day, and I give him water, too. You seen me. I don't call him names.

Eve die, and Adam die, and you know about their sons from turch, I imagine. But Amen keep on being alive: clopping around, eating grass when he find it, looking at the stars when it get dark out, thinking about stuff.

Sometimes he got catched, and that's when he was tie up and make to carry what somebody else din't want to carry plus more. And he plowed, too, but not with an ox but by himself, so it was harder, and it make him tired out.

Amen'd go to bed tired, but he wake up day after day after day.

Sometimes he'd run away and got to clop around and look at the stars. Most times, though, he couldn't even do that 'cause the rope was too tight.

Tons of times he was passed along. From one man

and his field to the next, Amen got so he din't even know who was lashing at his backside to get him to pull or carry or just because he was standing there. He din't try to talk to the men 'cause they was sore in the face and mad. They wake up day after day after day, too, but they got grey hairs and die, but when Amen was passed along, there was always somebody that was mad that had to wake up every day and work till dark.

And the fields got bigger 'cause there was more and more people to feed. When the fields got real big, the men start to lash each other. "I have mouths to feed!" they holler, and 'This is my land, my land! You get off!' they shout back and forth till their throats got as sore as their faces. They were mean to animals and mean to each other. The same tools they use to cut the animals and take their fur and eat them they use to fight with, for it worked the same in the end.

Everybody fight, and it was ugly. A man who grow crops in his field, he call it his territory. Poor Amen was stuck in it all. Even he was just a donkey, his big ears hear'd a lot and his eyes seen, too.

Pretty soon, the men figger four feet was better than two, so they took to ride Amen off their fields and into other men's fields, shouting "I have mouths to feed! This is my land now! You get off!"

Amen didn't much like that at all, so one day he stop still and didn't budge. "Move along!" the men say, but Amen say no (but not so anybody could hear it).

Did you know donkeys is stubborn? They are, so now you know why.

He stop at the edge of the field and wouldn't go no further. They push him. They shove him and fell.

A man can holler himself blind, is what Amen says. One man stomp the ground. Another yell at the sky.

"No," Amen say. "I won't go to the other fields with you."

What they was was strangers. All the people around him. All the people even in the other fields they try to take when it wasn't even theirs. Strangers like my best friend just in kindergarten become a stranger. Like Adam become a stranger. Amen might have knowed them but not anymore. He had clop around too much, and one lash become just like any other. He din't even know who was yelling at him this time.

Everyone was ugly, and he was ugly to them 'cause he was a stupid, dirty donkey that don't listen, was what they think.

The strangers hit him and hit him to get him to move along like I say, but they all the sudden give up 'cause they was just sick and tired of it all.

Amen got tie up tight, and the strangers go away to figger something else out, how to fill up their bellies, and Amen go to sleep. But when he wake up, he was fine again like he din't never get beat hard with a stick and a lash at the edge of a field that was already big enough anyways.

The first raindrop hit the roof of the barn like it wanted to be heard. The blunt smack was soon followed by others in quick succession.

"Rain, rain, go away," Chirp Vanhoosen sang as he joined Spring-baby in looking outward at the raindrops thudding onto the pasture ground. "Big, fat drops. Look at them come down."

Spring-baby had been leaning against the stall door opposite Chirp Vanhoosen. She had been close enough to the outside for her one arm to get a little wet, so she bounced her bottom off the stall door and rested further in. "I wouldn't have hit him either," she confessed. "And if I was Amen, I know I wouldn't have moved, not even if they lashed me hard."

"Even he's a donkey it still hurt."

"I don't understand, though. Why did everybody get so ugly? Didn't they know it wasn't nice to hit and steal?"

"Maybe," replied Chirp Vanhoosen. It was clear that he had considered these very questions by the way his eyes seemed to look inward for the answers. "But they was strangers, even to themselves. So if they know, they forget. Prob'ly din't know nothing but ugly. The grey hairs come before they think it over, most times, and by then, their bellies was full up. There was no reason to remember."

The raindrops were obese and steady, the givers dark, low, and generous. Puddles too young to be cloudy swelled about the pasture. Inside the barn was the constant roll of a bass drum: the rain faithfully beating the roof.

Spring-baby said, "You don't know where he went. It's coming down hard."

Chirp Vanhoosen smiled and stuck out his hand to catch the rainwater spilling off the eaves. "Rain makes the grass grow," he said. "And besides, this ain't nothing. Just wait. I'll tell you what I hear'd."

VIII

It come down so hard it about knocked the leaves from the trees, and it wasn't even fall. But not at first. The storm grow from something only little. Amen was tie to a bush when it first thunder, and he feel just a drop on his head but then two, then three, then a whole bunch more come down all over his body.

He get soak and wet. He hear'd "Ha, ha, ha" from everyone inside the house where the men and them lived.

He know the men wasn't laughing at him, though, 'cause before in the day when he was drag up a hill, the man who did it make fun of Noah 'cause he was up there finishing up the job. To Amen, what he seen look like

nothing he ever seen before: planks of wood build high
up and great big. Amen said it kinda look like a bucket
but make out of wood and long, and the water goes on
the outside. This is why the man laugh so hard at the
other man name Noah. And he wasn't the only one that
laugh 'cause there was a crowd and everyone make fun,
and I know how that feels. An ark is what it was named,
you see, and arks are make for oceans. But Noah was on
a hill, and there weren't no ocean for miles or a cloud in
the sky. He say he was told to make the ark. He say, "I'm
not bothering anybody, so go away."

You see, the man go out of his way to tease Noah.
He drag Amen up the hill because he could. No reason
but to be mean. The man only hear'd about Noah from
somebody else and Amen had to go 'cause the man say
he was a stupid, lazy donkey.

The crowd laugh while Noah was finishing up, and
they laugh all the way down the hill and right into
when it got dark. That's when Amen, he was tie to a
bush, and it start to cloud up and rain. Amen, he don't
like being out in the rain, but he'd rather get wet than
feel the lash and prob'ly get hit.

What I mean is, they was violent men. Always up
to no good, doing real bad every time the thought
come, like hitting people or touching everybody's pri-
vates.

The drops come but not big and fat, so what it was
was really a sprinkle but a steady one that got him wet.
Amen stand out by the bush, and he couldn't escape
'cause the knot was tie tight. He yank it hard, but that
couldn't even do it. So he just hang his head and give
up and think about how those men were even mean
and ugly to Noah that had two legs.

Amen watch the puddles grow on the ground as
best he could with the light that come out of the tent
where the men laugh. He think about stuff. He wish he

was free. When he lift up his head, though, to stretch his neck, he find that the rope that tie him to the bush was break apart like it was a sugar cube in water. Pieces of rope was just down there in the water and mud, and here Amen din't do nothing.

I know, I know. I look the same way and so did Amen at the pieces, but he din't look for long 'cause what he got was what he really think when he look at the puddles. That was the stuff I say. Let go. Away from the lash.

So he take off and din't look back. He splash out of the village and right on away into the dark, and he weren't afraid one bit like me or you prob'ly. He run and run, for he smell green grass but really taste it, and he feel the sun. But like I say, it was sprinkling steady. And he din't know where he was running to, but his four legs take him somewhere anyways. He run away, but run to something, *to* something.

"I know the story," Spring-baby interjected. "He's running to the ark. I already know what happens. You don't need to tell me."

Chirp Vanhoosen smiled, nodded patiently. Then he said, "But the story, we hear'd it from people that looks like me and you. That's what Amen tell me when I said I already know the story, too."

"But it's all the same."

"No," said Chirp Vanhoosen firmly.

"I don't understand."

"All what happens, all what ever happens, it's not all for those that have two legs."

"People."

Chirp Vanhoosen's smile widened. "Amen, he said that would shrink the story, make it tiny. That's what he tell me anyways when I ask what you ask."

Just then Spring-baby thought she detected a faint, embarrassed chuckle from the stable hand. She smiled tentatively, at which point Chirp Vanhoosen simply picked up the story where he left off.

When Amen run, he din't know what it mean, and he din't care what it mean—like I din't care either when I come home from school where they pick on me, and I run up that road you see there.

By the time he get tired out and just had to walk, Amen was way way aways and the sprinkle come harder. But he hardly pay any attention to it, for what his eyes couldn't see, his ears hear'd, 'cause like I say, they're big. All around him was sloshing and splashing—sometimes grunting, snorting, sometimes breathing loud. Was it a lion? He din't know. Or a dog? Or another donkey that's rope come apart like sugar?

In the valley where he was, the noises din't stop at all. He slosh along and hear lots of sloshing around him, and the way got steeper and steeper, and the noises just got closer and closer.

To the left, Amen see shapes and also to the right—big shapes and little shapes all going the same direction as him, sloshing, and splashing up 'cause they was climbing a hill. Pretty soon, the shapes that was dark and hard to see wasn't so dark and hard to see no more, for they was right next to him.

One shape turn out to be an elephant, a real live one that make real big splashes! And another was a camel, and another was a giraffe! Amen know them from where he was before when they shared the same stream for to get water. He din't think to ask where they been or nothing, 'cause when he turn to look the other direction, here there was another elephant and another camel and another giraffe. Amen was what you call in between two halfs of a zipper. Other animals come, too, on either side of him, but I'd be here all day saying what all of them was.

Everybody was soak and wet, but everybody din't care at all. It was like the bus just dropped them off at home, and who cares about rain?!

One time, though, Amen seen the lion that growled at him one time—you remember—walking along with sneaky little splashes. Amen got scared and even more scared when he seen the lion weren't by himself, but there was another lion sloshing along with him. Amen look and watch for to see teeth, but wouldn't you know it, that lion and the other lion just walk on by looking happy as can be like they could care less about some donkey in the rain.

And there was wolfs and panthers and tigers. But Amen say they din't bother with anybody either, just splosh, splosh, splosh.

At the top of the hill, they all make it, but they wasn't alone for there was Noah in front of his great big bucket with the door open and light inside for everybody to know where to go.

Amen's four legs take him right up to the door, too, like the other animals, and he try to go in, but Noah—who was picked on like me and Amen—he say, "Stop!"

The elephants pass. The camels pass.

"Donkey, you are alone," say Noah.

Amen look left and right then down at his hooves like he did when he watch the puddles grow by the bush.

The wolfs pass. The lions pass. The kangaroos hop in 'cause they was there with them.

And the rain got to be fat, and it come down harder, and Amen just want to go inside like the others.

"Donkey, this is not supposed to be," say Noah. "Where is the female of your kind?"

Amen din't lift up his head 'cause he din't even know.

Then Noah say when he look up at the storm clouds, "All the men, all the creatures …" And when Amen did lift up his head again, Noah look like he was sorry for him: "Even you, and I saw the man whip your back." That's what Noah say to him when he look down at Amen feeling bad.

The sounds from the great big bucket was like the crowdest zoo, for that's what it was. Mooing and barking and roaring and neighing. Trumpeting like the elephants do. Crows going *caw, caw.* Kittens going *meow.* And the monkeys yelling, *ooh, ooh, ooh.*

Did you know what a donkey does is bray? Sounds like *he-haw, he-haw*—real high then real low.

He-haw! come from out in the dark where there wasn't no light.

"Here's the female of your kind, donkey," say Noah.

What Amen seen when he turn around was a donkey like him but a girl that was soak and wet and muddy 'cause of the slop on the ground. She splosh into where they could see her and right up to Amen like she know him all along.

"It will be better for us all," say Noah, and then what he did was let Amen and the girl donkey in. And then they got their own stall but not like here 'cause where they was they had to share just one.

The rain come down even more and more, and the drops got as fat as fists, and only after some time not real long, something make the stall move to where Amen and the girl donkey got wobbly legs. Back and forth, it feel, and up and down, up and down like on the teeter-totter at the playground.

He hear'd the loud water come down really a lot on

the water already outside. He hear'd *caw, caw,* and the mooing what cows do, and the howling, and the barking, and the roars that are lions but not only them. And what else was pounding on the bucket from outside and hollering like "Help!" and "Save us!" but what Amen did was eat the grass that Noah give him 'cause them on the outside wasn't the boss of him no more.

IX

The way the downpour finally ended was the way many tantrums end: the clouds, a child, still grumbling but spent. The pasture had been doused in tears. The tears had awakened the muggy sweet smells of early summer.

Spring-baby said, "They floated for a long time. I know that."

"Amen hear'd banging on the outside for only a few days but no more after a little while. The rain fall and fall. Pretty soon all he ever hear'd was rain and the animals inside."

"But it eventually stopped raining, and there was the dove. When did the dove come with the olive branch?"

"Amen din't say nothing about a branch."

"The dove brought the olive branch is what I learned. That was how Noah found out that the water was going away."

Chirp Vanhoosen scrunched up his face, searched his

memory, found nothing. "It was the drop that tell him. I dunno about a dove."

"A drop?"

"Like that," Chirp Vanhoosen said. He was looking at a row of droplets hurrying to gorge themselves from the water trickling off the roof. "But one," he continued. "One drop that hang from a beam and grow fat and heavy, but it din't even fall."

"I don't understand."

"Me, too, till Amen tell me you don't need a mouth for to say something."

"Water takes, water gives." That's what the drop tell Amen still when the ark was creaking 'cause of the back and forth and the up and down.

Maybe 'cause he's a donkey he look straight up and not around like prob'ly you and me, but there he was just staring at the drop that look like it was gonna fall it was so big, but it din't. Noah was a good builder, but the rain come so much, and some of it got in and stay when the waves splash. There was other drops, but they got fat and fall down. So why don't this one as big as his nose fall, he din't know, and he din't know how it talk either.

"Water takes, water gives," it say again, and Amen just stand there 'cause where could he go.

Then what the drop say was, "It is enough. The clay will rise from the deep."

Now the drop talk quiet, what Amen say. And it wasn't the sound of a grownup man or even a lady. What it sound like was a kid like you but the way Amen tell, prob'ly littler. It was a kid's voice that whisper about the water. The drop din't let go of the beam, even the floodwater outside hit the ark.

Amen think, then he say, "The world is covered in water."

"I have covered the world, yes."

"You have taken many."

"The wicked have all perished."

Amen say he snort when he hear'd that, for he got lash a lot by mean men, and what the drop say make him glad.

But the drop, it seem to know what Amen think 'cause it say, "You will come to dread again, donkey. You will fear as you have feared before."

"I will be lashed?"

"Yes."

"I will be beaten?"

"Yes."

"But why, if the wicked are gone?"

The drop, it shake like what you do when you cry. Then it say, "There is one more stubborn than you."

Amen tell the drop he was afraid.

"Water takes, water gives," say the drop right back, then it got real great big and plop right down on top of Amen's head.

And after that the other donkey that was the girl brayed but not 'cause the drop hit Amen. There was moving all about till suddenly there wasn't, for what happened was solid ground. The ark, it got stuck. The elephants trumpet 'cause they trip. The lions roar, for they fall a little, too. Everybody was so used to the big bucket moving about, they din't know what to do when they was still.

Amen's head was still wet when Shem, that was Noah's son, run by hollering and carrying on about the solid ground. Amen think about what the drop tell him. He never like the lash. He hurt a lot by the end of the day. But the drop sound nice; what he tell me, if words were oats, that's what them words were to him.

Everybody need to have the stink blow off of them. They been bobbing around, just bobbing around on the water for a really real long time. Even when the rain stop coming, finally, the water was as endless as the sky. That's what Amen find out from the squirrels and the raccoons that could see better. So nobody got too excited anymore, but that was after about a week of blue sky.

When the ark at last hit the ground, more windows was opened. Like the rain done on the outside, the fresh air done on the inside, it come pouring in. Eagles stretch out their wings to catch the air and so did hawks and parrots. Kitties sniff at it, and hyenas laugh like they do. Dogs whine 'cause they want to go out. Bears claw the wood. Horses whinny and stamp the ground hard. Men and women laugh. Their kids tug at their clothes.

Noah take a long time for to build the ark, so he only say, "Good." Then he go down to feed and water the animals.

They live tilted like that for a while. Everybody inside figger how to get about on an angle 'cause, see, the ground where the ark was sticking was uneven. Noah and his sons give food and water to the animals every day like before. The squirrels could see the tops of the mountains more and more come out of the water that was like sky.

One day, though, Amen hear'd something they all hear'd only once before, and that was the bolt on the door. Only it wasn't closing up but opening, for Noah say that he seen most of the mountains now. The stalls and cages was open next and out of the ark everybody run or fly or hop or crawl and spill all over the dry land. They was like seeds to the wind; they was like a sneeze when you don't put your hand over your mouth.

Shem wasn't the only son 'cause there was Japheth and Ham, too. They all of them had wives and kids and there was plenty of them: lots of mouths to feed.

Japheth say, "The world is big. It is good again, Father."

"It was always so," say Noah.

Then Ham tell them all, "It is much to rule—all of it before us. It is well for my family. I pray it will be well with yours."

And that's when Amen, he feel a hand on his mane, clutching, holding, and when he try to walk away, do you know what, he couldn't.

"They wouldn't let him," Spring-baby said, adding to the story.

"He was back carrying things that day, and he couldn't even go nowhere."

Spring-baby looked again at the harness and coil of rope hanging from the hook on the support beam and found that these items—the harness and the rope—which were formerly just part of the unassuming milieu of the barn, now silently articulated their function: to keep, to subdue, to bind, to control. She returned her gaze to Chirp Vanhoosen. But her imagination allowed her to see only the shapeless form of him because a sad, laden donkey was in the way.

"Even Amen wasn't the only one," continued Chirp Vanhoosen, equally consumed.

"Why?"

Chirp Vanhoosen heard ancient screams—saw blood, smelled smoke, too. "What's worse is Noah kill another animal," he said. "And he burn him all up."

"Burned him?"

"It's what Noah did. The other take Amen."

This was the only explanation Chirp Vanhoosen offered, so Spring-baby simply joined him as he stood mesmerized, imagining that fire. They didn't budge nor did they speak until Fafa summoned Spring-baby from the fence.

"Okay," Spring-baby called back. She left Chirp Vanhoosen to wonder alone about the orange flickers, the crackles, the snaps.

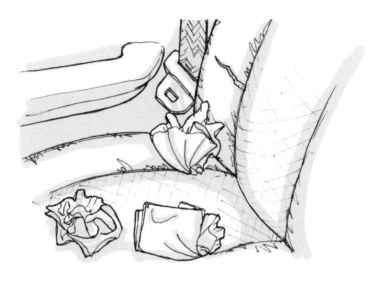

X

Emblazoned in green on the large window in front of Lorelei were the words *Minter's Service Station*. She was in Virginia—she was sure of that, at least—but everything else in her universe only amounted to what her senses could readily perceive. She had been driving for a long time, and she was well off any interstate. Her stomach was growling, and her butt was sore. She had just put gas into the station wagon and was absently still holding the nozzle inside the neck of the gas tank. She was talking to the dead. She was stupefied by God.

"Usually I'd take care of that, but I'm a little backed up in the garage." It was a graying man with a kindly face who interrupted. He sauntered up to her, wiping his hands on a rag and smiling broadly. On his button-up shirt was a patch that read *Mister Minter*. "I can look at that tire, though," he said. Then he readjusted his flat-billed cap and kneeled by the front passenger-side tire.

Lorelei saw immediately what he was talking about. A bulge the size of a grapefruit explained the bumping sensation she'd been ignoring for the past few miles.

"Dangit!" she grumbled.

"Won't take but a half hour," said Mister Minter. "It ain't safe as it is. I've seen this plenty of times before. I can fit you in quick so you can be on your way."

"How much for a new tire?"

Mister Minter stood up slowly, grimaced as he did some figuring. "Oh," he groaned thoughtfully. "I gotta re-tread in the garage. I'll cut you a deal."

Lorelei finally replaced the nozzle.

"Payphone's over there if you need it. You don't want to drive another mile on a tire like that."

She agreed that she didn't. In fact, she didn't want to drive anywhere anymore. Spinning wheels exhausted her; flight exhausted her. She had been pleading with a tight-lipped lover two days in the ground, yet no matter how much she cajoled or how much she screamed, Mike was a smoking wick seconds after a puff took the flame. He was as mute as the gravestone that bore his name. Lorelei could no longer tolerate the only voice being her own.

She walked to the payphone and dialed zero before she knew how she was going to explain herself.

Fafa had just trudged into the house when the phone rang. He had discovered that he didn't want to be at the office either. "Hello," he said after he accepted the charges.

"It's me."

"It's about time you turned up. Where have you been?"

"Driving."

"Driving? Driving where? How can a mother just up and

leave? And what about Mom and me?"

"I'm sorry. I need to speak to Spring-baby."

"Turn around from wherever you are and get back here."

"Please. Spring-baby."

"You're not the only one!"

"My daughter, please!"

Fafa thought into the phone, then after a moment said, "Hold on."

He called for her throughout the house until he remembered Spring-baby telling them about the donkey. After he retrieved her, he sat breathing heavily in a kitchen chair, not trying to hide the fact that he was listening in.

"Mom."

"Hello, honey."

"Where are you? Why did you go?"

"I'm sorry. I'm sorry I left you like that."

"When are you coming back?"

Lorelei answered with a hesitant, sputtering sigh.

"Mom?"

"I'm looking for butterflies," Lorelei confessed weakly.

"Mom?"

"You were only a baby when my grandmother passed away, so you probably don't remember much. She was a beautiful, good-hearted woman with hair braided down past the middle of her back. Sometimes she would let me and my sisters brush it."

"I remember the pictures."

"That's right. I showed you the pictures. She used to watch me and my sisters every afternoon when Mom and Dad were at work. Every other Sunday it seemed we'd all have lunch or dinner at her house. I was with her in that house when she died. I was brushing back her hair when she went. It was sunrise on a Sunday, and I had the curtains pulled back so she could look out. I said, 'Look, Gramma. Look at how red it is.'

"She looked at where I was pointing, but do you know what she said? She said, 'Aren't the butterflies pretty? Look at how they rise with the sun.' And that's when she died. Her body relaxed as the sunlight slowly grew brighter on her face."

"What were they? Was there really butterflies in the room?"

"None that I could see," Lorelei replied. Then she gathered the courage to say what she was working up to. "But I learned that it wasn't important that I seen them. What was important was that she told me they were there at all."

"The butterflies were there."

"The butterflies were for me. Your dad didn't leave me with any butterflies. I slept in the car last night, but I haven't felt them yet. Please be patient with your mother."

Spring-baby held the receiver to her mouth with both hands now. "There's a donkey in the pasture. The man that takes care of him is Chirp Vanhoosen. He knew Dad a long time ago."

"Your dad had a lot of friends."

"The donkey's name is Amen."

"Amen for a donkey."

"He's older than death."

Lorelei didn't say anything for a moment. "I know how much it hurts, your dad being gone," she said finally. "Please don't be mad at me for leaving you there. It's only for a short while. Not forever." Then she reminded her daughter how much she loved her, returned the receiver to its hook, and wept without letting go.

Spring-baby hung up, too.

"Gone again? When is she coming back?" Fafa spoke up, annoyed.

"Butterflies," replied Spring-baby.

"Butterflies?"

She told Fafa about the butterflies and the sunrise as best as she could recall.

The aging physician eyed her intently throughout the retelling. "Is that what this is about?" he snapped when she finished.

"I told her about Amen."

But he was searching this way and that for the answer to his own question, his tired head lolling slightly as if it were loosely fitted to the rest of his body. Eventually, he just stared blankly ahead. "I've been homesick for years. And with Mike now gone, I'm all the sicker: Each day I'm given gets stranger and more lonesome than the last."

From where she stood, Spring-baby spied Granny's ghost slip into the bathroom. The can of air freshener hissed. The ghost locked the door.

Fafa looked up at her. "This is your first time away like this, isn't it? I mean without your mother."

Spring-baby had once convinced her parents to let her stay the night at a friend's house. With her friend she rode the school bus way out into the countryside where dejected, unsightly dwellings were tucked into the landscape. Spring-baby helped when water for cooking had to be fetched from an outside pump. She learned that she had to pee outside over a hole and that everybody shared a bedroom—the five kids, a bed. When darkness settled and bedtime arrived, though, Spring-baby lost the nerve to sleep next to poor strangers.

She nodded that it was.

He cleared his throat. "I was five years old when my dad died," he said, the words tumbling unrehearsed from his mouth. "I remember standing in front of the gurney with my mother and an old black orderly. We were by the elevator. The sheet over my dad covered everything but the very top of his head, so what I saw was a white shape with brown hair like mine used to be. The black orderly must've been a nice man because he leaned down to me and said, 'Do you see that elevator? I'm going to put your daddy in there, press a button, and send him to heaven.'"

"That's a nice man," said Spring-baby.

"Yes," Fafa agreed. "It was the only explanation I got. My mother took to the bottle and started going out every night after that. She'd leave me. I was five. I ended up in an orphanage, which was just as well."

"She didn't come for you?"

He was shaking his head before Spring-baby finished the question. "People go away. They die. They walk out, which in the end, is the same as dying anyway. And all of the sudden, you're at an age when you know more people who've left than who're still around. You become sad; that's fine. That's one word for it. But I tell you a better word is homesickness. You wake up in the same house you've been waking up in for twenty odd years. You have the same job, the same office. People around town know you and you, them. But none of these people is your mom. None of these people is your dad—your dad or your son. If we're lucky, God gives us an old black man and a white lie. Your mom wants butterflies? Butterflies? She has you. As for me, I'm older. I'm a living memory to you. You'll see. When you're my age, you'll wonder where everyone has gone."

"Where has everyone gone?"

Fafa removed his glasses and pinched the bridge of his corpulent nose. "On an elevator," he said then he let the tears come more freely. His shoulders shook. He bent his head down.

The bathroom door creaked open. Granny stepped out but only glanced at her husband before retreating to the bedroom she had been sharing with him for the same twenty odd years.

XI

Kevin and Jesus had their own thing going. When the news of his brother's imminent passing finally circumnavigated the deaf ear he turned, Jesus gave him medical school so he could learn the secrets of what it is for the body to die. Kevin was certain of this purpose: to know that systems shut down one by one, to know that the living mechanism becomes a motionless object, having surrendered its name with its warmth, its soul with its place among the living. Were it not for science, Kevin would be crippled with melancholy. He regularly talked out loud to Jesus and thanked Him for logic. In the sanctuary of his Volkswagon Beetle parked for the last half hour in his parents' driveway, Kevin concluded another prayer and capped the flask of bourbon he always kept in the glove compartment.

He had been preparing to rejoin his parents in the com-
munal procession through the valley of the shadow of his
brother's death. A couple of hours earlier, he had left his sister
Marissa's little apartment just off campus at the University of
Louisville. She had the busyness of summer classes to rescue
her, and besides, her feet were exhausted from the drudgery
of sorrow.

In the casket was a vessel, he thought. Bereft of name. No
longer a son, a brother, a father, a husband. A system ceased.
Kevin put his hand on the lever that would let the world
flood in should he pull it. He removed his hand, though, and
uncapped the flask instead.

"Jesus is savior," he said before taking another snort. His
own vessel received the salve with a jitter that was quickly
suppressed.

Next to him, Mike, dressed in the suit in which he was
buried, said, "Yes, He is" and somewhere in the tiny backseat,
Jesus chimed "Yes, I am."

This was precious knowledge to Kevin. It sustained him,
gave him perspective. The world is fallen, he thought, and dying
begins as soon as we are conceived. Only the Son can save us,
but for now, we get textbooks and professors, and if we are
lucky, days when the futility of the present isn't so oppressive.

Jesus saves, thought Kevin with gratitude, but science
explains: birth, death, the identifiable cycle of living and dying,
conveniently expressed and manageable.

Not too long ago, the mystery of the great *Why* had stolen
upon and squashed him, leaving him a mute, grasping idiot.
It happened when he realized there were more questions than
answers—somewhere between the elongation of his chubby
body into something leaner and getting smacked with the
realization that most people didn't care that he was the son of
someone important.

He asked, "Where did I come from?" and the answer he

was given was that he came from his parents, and before them, God. Then he asked, "Where will I go?" and the answer he received was to heaven if you're good. He looked all around him. He touched his nose, rubbed his arm. He looked at the body that was his and concluded that it was his for now, having realized that the only world he knew had a beginning he could not remember and an ending he could not fathom.

In the end, all that was left was to examine the moving, tangible parts of the inescapably mortal Homo-sapiens and to make do, madly clinging to the hope of future rescue, the promise of everlasting life.

Even the donkey agreed to a point, but after that, there was a difference of opinion. The donkey thought one way, but Kevin thought quite the opposite. And it didn't help matters that Kevin became increasingly unwilling to listen. As he got older, grew up, the donkey's voice became easier to ignore, so much so that there came a day when all Kevin heard was braying, and it was that day that marked his last to visit the pasture.

On that evening the sun had dropped behind a distant knoll, and the forms of the day—trees, houses, and such—were just beginning to lose their distinction, becoming softer, more pliable as if preparing to eventually recede into the coming night. Kevin was at his usual place on the fence. There was no reason anymore to go into the barn. The donkey knew he would come, and they had long ago tacitly agreed to meet in the open.

The donkey appeared slowly from the barn: no hurry, clopping along, his head bouncing easily with his stride. "Kevin," he said when he reached the fence. "Another day and you'd be a stranger. Where have you been? We used to talk every day."

"I have college to think about," said Kevin. "It's more than I ever thought: application forms, letters of recommendation, all that stuff. I have to think about my future. I have to make something of myself."

"What is it you would like to learn?"

"I want to be a physician like my dad. It will take me a long time. I want to be respected and make money.

"Certainly," replied the donkey. "It is good to help others."

"I think I can become a successful physician."

The donkey swished away a fly with his tail and didn't speak for a moment. Then he said, "Let me ask you this though: How do you want to grow? Following in your father's footsteps is fine, but if you see becoming a physician as a destination, then I fear you will miss your purpose."

"Purpose?" returned the young man. "My purpose is clear. I am to grow up, and I am to earn a living."

"Is this what you think of as growth?"

"As a physician, I will learn how the body works."

"Yes," said the donkey. "The thing we inhabit needs its maintenance. The boy in the white house feeds me and gives me water every day. What I am talking about is the walk you're on, not the hat you wear."

Kevin was now tall enough to shelve his arms on one of the posts. He looked behind him at the house grown dim before he caught the eyes of the donkey. "We have been talking for a long time. You have told me stories that have kept me thinking and wondering for days. But you are a donkey—an old one for sure— but a donkey all the same, and I am a person. No boy will come to me with food and water. If I don't eat, I will die sooner than later. I was not given what you were given. My body will fail. The body I will feed will fail. You have a luxury I do not."

"But you do."

"How? Since I've known you, I've changed: my body, my voice. It doesn't stop."

"It is good to change. It is right to change."

"I would think you'd see," said the young man, kicking agitatedly at the bottom of the post. "I will see my hair turn gray. I will watch as my skin wrinkles, my shoulders stoop. I am trapped by this fate. I cannot escape it: this life with days that are numbered."

The donkey bobbed his head, obviously irritated. "Have you not listened to a word I said? Everything is brief but God. Even decay. Even as far as you can possibly look into the future. God is certainly bigger than the here and now. What I've been sharing with you is not meant to be understood. It is meant to be accepted. It is a gift, a means by which you can be liberated. You may learn how the body works—know it as a machine, a temporary carrier—but what good is this knowledge if you see yourself as a prisoner?"

"I am a prisoner of this body."

"You are much more than the flesh."

"I will know how the body works. I will know my adversary. You haven't known my fear."

"*He-haw!*" said the donkey. He shuffled a bit out of his stance to find a better, more helpful view of the young man in front of him. "You cannot go it alone. If you take anything from a donkey, take this warning from me. *He-haw! He-haw!*"

"Someday Jesus will save me," said Kevin.

The sun was nothing more than a few lingering rays, and the donkey had grown hazy: a shape as nebulous as the future Kevin foresaw.

"He already has. *He-haw! He-haw!*"

Kevin was through with the animal. He turned and walked back through the yard and up to the house, leaving the donkey in the dark, in the idealism of youth.

Years later, he stared blankly at the same house from his little car.

In the window, Spring-baby stood watching and waiting for her uncle to move. When he finally did, when he finally pulled the lever and let the world surge in, Spring-baby let fall the curtains she had pulled back, hoping she was not seen, wondering if the look of strain and suffering on her uncle's face had anything to do with her dad.

XII

My mother is looking for butterflies," said Spring-
baby. She was back at the barn. She had fled from
the house and the woe it contained.

Chirp Vanhoosen was there where she had left him as if
he were just biding his time for Spring-baby to return so he
could resume the story. Of course, more than likely he attended
to some minor chores in her absence, but Spring-baby hadn't
bothered to notice or even to ask. She had slipped through the
barbed wire fence, scampered into the barn, and said what she
had to say with no more than a hello as preface.

"I like butterflies," said Chirp Vanhoosen. "I seen one like
a leaf turn'd in the fall, but the leaves were still green. I try to
catch it, but I'm glad I din't."

"I told Mom about Amen and death and all."

"That donkey still ain't show up." He looked from side to side, expecting, maybe, that the donkey would show up right then and there to spite him.

"Is he ever homesick?" asked Spring-baby seriously, for it was the question that had been pushing toward the surface since Fafa unwittingly planted the seed.

"Homesick for what?" Chirp Vanhoosen replied. "The stream? The grass? The lion that would never have bite him?"

"He's an old donkey," said Spring-baby.

"Older than—"

"Old enough to always be by himself no matter how hard he tried."

Chirp Vanhoosen chewed on her words for a moment but found them a bit sour. He said gently, "God is a loving God."

"My mother is looking for butterflies," repeated Spring-baby. "What is a butterfly? I don't know what one is. If Fafa had one, would he be happy? Is that what Granny looks for in the bathroom in all that smoke? If I had one, would I be able to see my dad? Amen's old."

"Yes," said Chirp Vanhoosen.

"I'm only twelve. I feel homesick already."

Chirp Vanhoosen tapped the toe of one boot on the heel of the other, more out of thought than to rid the boot of the dirt caked into the tread. "What is a butterfly, like what you said?"

Spring-baby took her time to answer. "Something good," she said finally. "Something to look forward to. I think Amen must wonder where everybody went because that's like what I wonder, too."

"Where did everybody go to?"

"My dad is dead. It's not going to get any better. I think my mom is looking for something made up."

"The butterflies?"

"What butterflies did Amen get? People made him work all

day long, like you said, and they sometimes hit him. That was what he woke up to. Those people who did that, he watched come and go, but there were people like Noah who were glad Amen didn't have to drown. He went, too. Dead like Dad. Amen was left alone. Why do we get left alone, and it's not even because of anything we did?"

Chirp Vanhoosen did not have a ready answer. He pulled himself up from a slump but soon thereafter deflated back into his normal posture. The girl had stumped him. "Amen, he work alright," he began hesitantly, not knowing exactly where the thought might take him. "He wake up every day with something to do. Maybe he was lonesome or homesick is what you said. But maybe being busy take his mind off of it or even being busy was good enough for a friend."

Spring-baby stood silent, dumbfounded, jaw growing steadily agape, a tear ripening in the corner of an eye. "What kind of love is that?" she submitted weakly.

"God's," replied Chirp Vanhoosen. Then he shifted his weight uneasily from one leg to the other.

Amen work from sunup till dark always with somebody around telling him what to do. It wasn't different from before it flood and drown the world. Amen'd get up and do what he was tell to do and every now and then look over his shoulder to see if the face is different. It was always a gruff, twisted face—dirty, sweaty, sometimes mean but always determine like me when I know I have to do my chores every day.

One time, though, Amen learn a name.

"I know your name is Abraham," say Amen, but Abraham wasn't listening, for he was working real hard himself. So Amen turn his head as much as he could. He was in a field pulling a plow, and he want to try again for to get Abraham to listen, so he say, "You work hard, too, and you are old like me."

"Move along, donkey," say Abraham. "The sun is pink in the sky, and there is more yet to do."

The next day early in the morning when Abraham come out to him, Amen, he say, "Is it better for you?"

But Abraham still din't say nothing. Even he din't take Amen to the field either but put on him a saddle for to go on a trip with two helpers. Isaac come, too. Isaac's mom was name Sarah, and she think one time how she can't ever have a child at all for she was so old, but she was wrong.

Abraham look real sad. What Amen say they go to was Moriah on a mountaintop high up, and when they finally get there, Abraham take his son off of Amen and tie Amen to a tree. He tell the helpers to stay with Amen while him and Isaac was going to walk a little bit aways from where they was all standing. Abraham take the cut wood he bring and what he did was put it on Isaac, and Abraham take the knife and some fire with him when they finally go on up. When Abraham and Isaac was out of sight, the helpers plop down on the ground and sleep 'cause they was tired out from all the walking.

Amen wasn't standing there prob'ly five minutes when he hear from behind him some twigs snap like somebody was stepping on them.

"*Baa-aah!*" come a voice, and when Amen turn around, he seen a ram walk up towards him from out of the bushes. His fur was white, and his thick horns curl around his head. "I have walked my whole life to be here this day. My feet are tired. Is the boy near?"

"The boy is with his father. They walked away not too long ago."

The ram, he was panting for the mountain it was a steep one. "Good," say the ram. "My journey is almost done. I have come to bring what I was given to bring."

Amen, he look at the ram and seen nothing, not even around his neck.

The ram fold his front legs beneath him like what they do if you ever seen a ram go to sit down then let his rump take the rest of his body to the ground on a small patch of grass. "There is time to catch my breath," say the ram. "I will finish my journey when I'm told."

"When you're told?" say Amen.

"When I know what I carry."

I imagine Amen shake the shrub he was tied to 'cause he bob his head up and down not knowing what to think.

"I see how old you are," say the ram. "Why are you troubled?"

Amen tell him how long it's been since he eat good grass—so long that it feel like he must've dream it.

The ram nodded like he know what Amen talk about. "The grass has been bad for me, too," he say as he nibble on the grass right in front of his mouth. "At one time, I believe, the grass tasted good. But when I began to sprout horns, I filled my belly but was never satisfied."

"This is how I live," say Amen.

"This is how we all have come to live," say the ram. "Perhaps this is why I left the comfort of the fold: to find the good—"

All of the sudden, the ram shut up. He sniff the air and move his head from side to side like maybe he was onto something. Then real quick he lean forward and stick out his hind legs like rams do to get up, if you've ever seen a ram get up, and out come his front hooves and up he go. "*Baa-aah! Baa-aah!*" he cry and run up where Abraham and Isaac was before Amen could say a word.

Well, the rope come loose when Amen jerk his head to look at where the ram run off. He din't go after him or nothing, for he wouldn't know what to do anyways if he catch up. So he just stay there and think about what the ram say. Good grass. Bad grass. The thing he bring. Amen bob his head up and down again for he still din't know, but when he bite into the same spot of grass that the ram was on, he think then that maybe he might. The grass was so good that he din't even notice when Abraham come back down the mountain with Isaac.

Spring-baby spoke up before the last note of the story had a chance to fade away. "I know what happened to the ram. He got his horns caught in the bushes, and when Abraham saw him, he killed him instead of Isaac."

"The ram got stab, and he got burnt up, too," Chirp Vanhoosen added.

"I think that's mean," said Spring-baby.

"Why?" Chirp Vanhoosen returned. It was a knee-jerk response.

"What did the ram do? He didn't deserve to die. That's what I've been saying all along."

"He walk a long, long ways."

"To get killed and not Isaac."

"All by himself on the mountaintop what Amen tell me."

The two relaxed into a meditative silence. Chirp Vanhoosen wondered what he could say next. Spring-baby irksomely worked on making a divot in the ground with her heel.

"It isn't fair," she said finally.

Chirp Vanhoosen agreed, but he didn't know how to say so just yet, so in the end, he decided not to utter a word. Instead, he pulled up a dented, wooden stool used, more than likely, for allowing somebody to reach up into high places, and sat down with a faint grunt, bony knees projecting outward, giving him the look of a jeans-wearing, barn-dwelling frog. It was then that he gave some thought to Spring-baby's proclamation. He pinched his nostrils and gave his nose a rub with his knuckle then fiddled with the exposed hem of his grungy shirt. Then he said simply, "It ain't. But Amen never come across any way but 'greeable even though he walk long enough to get miffed if he really want to."

XIII

T he ram, he din't have nothing on Amen, really, like what I say to you about him walking a long, long ways. The ram was born and grow for to walk up the mountain that time when him and Amen meet. But Amen, he had other places to go. So that's what he did, and he seen rams come and go, and sometimes he was left all alone with only faces that sometimes had names."

He know being real tired, but he know getting up the next day feeling better. Up with the sun, he done what work he had to do, but the way he tell it to me, he never think past the sun going down 'cause, who knows, it might be different the next day. I guess that

can help anybody be 'greeable. Just don't get bog down
with thinking about tomorrow and even more the day
after that.

I imagine he have his days like anybody, though.
Sometimes the load he was make to carry was too heavy
or even the road was too long no matter how much
he wish it wasn't, and it was all he could do to keep
it between the horizons. But Amen what he had was
practice at how to live 'cause, 'member what I say? I say
Amen live hundreds of lives when we only get just one.

Moses live to be a hundred and twenty years old,
but to Amen he was just a kid that even he live a whole
bunch he could see and move good anyways. But he
seen a lot of tomorrow and because of that, he got sad
and scared when he finally find his own thing he had
to carry. It wasn't a drop like what talk to Amen. It was
like that but different.

A bush on fire. That's what talk to Moses, only it
wasn't really a bush but something bigger. Moses come
back from what he was doing, which was shepherding,
and tell Amen all about it 'cause a donkey won't think
you're crazy when you say a bush on fire give you a
chore to do.

"Donkey, you are so unlike the rest of your kind,"
say Moses when he come back down from the mountain that the bush on fire was on and nobody was
around. "You were a good trade. Others dig their
hooves into the dirt and refuse to budge, but not you.
Where I lead, you follow."

Amen snort when Moses give him a pat.

"Today, the God of my fathers spoke to me from a
bush that was not consumed by fire. I am to return to
Egypt. I am to speak to Pharaoh directly. The God of
my fathers says I am to lead my people from misery.
He has given me the power to convince, but the truth is
that I still feel there must be a better man than me. My

speech is poor. I am as simple as the sheep I tend. Were I as sure as you, I could stand up to the task."

You prob'ly think like I did that Amen talk right there and then to Moses, but he din't. One talking surprise is enough for a day, Amen tell me, so he think it just be nice to listen 'cause sometimes that's just better anyways. So that's what he did, and that was a good thing, for Moses had more to get off his chest.

"Who am I?" Moses go on. "I am but flesh and bone, unimpressive. I am a coward, really. I fled from Pharaoh, vowing never to return, but I have been given a different fate, and quite truthfully, donkey, the weight of it is almost unbearable. How am I fit to be a leader of the Israelites? Why did God choose me when he could have chosen someone stronger, someone brighter, someone gifted with attributes I could only dream of possessing? Look at me, donkey."

Amen look.

"I can make my hand leprous by putting it into my cloak, and I can restore my hand just the same. I can turn water from the Nile into blood when I pour it out onto the ground. This staff you see: I can make it into a snake if I toss it before me."

Sure enough, Amen tell me, Moses fling his staff to the ground, and just like that, it was a snake till he pick it up again, and then it was back as a staff. That make Amen happy 'cause he's like me: He don't like snakes either.

Moses go on again: "I have been given these signs to do the Lord's work, yet though the Lord's anger burned against me when I asked for someone to be sent in my stead, I confess to you and the stars above that I am still afraid, so very afraid of what might be." Then he say, "Who am I but a simple man?" and he show Amen the top of his gray head.

Moses, he was a good man to Amen, so when

Amen seen him what it look like crying, he feel like
crying, too. He know he was scared. He know just how
it feel to hafta do what you don't even think you can do
like how can I even do it if I try my hardest. Amen, he
live hundreds of lives, but nobody say that was easy, for
when you live that long, you have tons of time to ask
why. That's what Amen did. Ask why a lot.

Moses lift up his head, though, when Amen want
to say something, but he din't get the chance to say
nothing. "I have never gone without," Moses say then,
and what Amen tell me, he even laugh some. "It is
not for us to know the ways of God. My eyes work
and so do my ears, and from my mouth, words can
come though until now they have never been eloquent.
God knows what I cannot know. And this must be
the end of it. It must. You are a good listener, donkey.
Tomorrow, I shall saddle you for the journey to Egypt."

On the next day, Moses did saddle him and he
pack up everything he had. He take his wife and sons.
Everything and everything. He walk right along with
Amen, and he held that staff the whole way there.
Where they was was Midian, but then they left 'cause
Moses had to go to Egypt to turn his staff into a snake.
Amen carry a lot that time, but that was okay, he tell
me, for to leave a place and go on a long trip when
you don't even know if you'll ever get back, a lot of
stuff is needed.

Moses din't talk much all the way there. What it
was, Amen say, was like he was listening: the wind blow
across the desert, and Amen catch the gist with his
big ears but not all the words that was in the wind.
But anyways, they was good words what he could hear,
and Amen say that Moses walk more and more like he
know where he was going.

I don't have a brother, but Moses did, so Aaron
come too, that was Moses's brother that meet them

along the way. Aaron speak good. He help Moses out,
but still it take a while for to make Pharaoh say yes
about the people getting freed. Even the people, the
Israelites, got mad at Moses and Aaron 'cause the Pharaoh make it hard on them when Moses and Aaron
keep on asking and wouldn't stop. Amen, he wait the
whole time. He even tell me how there was frogs and
bugs and hail as big around as my fist, but he din't get
restless too much 'cause, for one, he was inside where it
was safe and, two, those words he catch in the desert
like I say was good for him, too. And that's what he
think about, even when the bugs pile up outside and
the hail sound like thunder on the rooftop.

You ever see a donkey run? I have. So when Amen
tell me how they all run from Pharaoh, I know what it
prob'ly look like. *Cloppity, cloppity, cloppity, cloppity.*

What happen was, the Pharaoh—he was the king
of Egypt—finally said yes, but not till something
happen that Amen din't know. Only one night there
was a lot of crying real loud, and that night Pharaoh
got together with Moses and Aaron and say get out
of here. So they did. But that Pharaoh all the sudden
must've change his mind 'cause here they was walking
along and the next thing you know they got chase
by a whole army. That's when Amen run. That's when
everybody run.

Cloppity, cloppity, that's how it sounds. The whole
bunch run, and there was other donkeys, too, besides
Amen for to carry the gold they all take when they
leave Egypt.

Amen, he tell me what a staff is also use for 'cause
what Moses did was he had to raise it in his hand high
up and one day there's the sea and the next it's dry land
for to walk on. Amen seen lots of stuff—seen the sea
even come crashing back down on the Egyptians—but
he don't know what to make of any of it, and even he

walk with the people around the desert for forty years after that and think on all he seen every day, but he still don't know.

XIV

Sometimes Spring-baby would expose her bare leg from underneath the covers, letting the night air—like cool, delicious water—wash over her skin well enough for her to want to snuggle her leg back beneath the blankets, hoping that the equally soothing comforts of coolness and warmth would take her to the world she most desired.

She was in her aunt's old bed again, and a leg was dipped in the night air, yet when she eventually pulled it in to herself and the warmth her little body generated, her condition remained static: sleep was as reticent as a poor conversationalist. She even put a pillow between her legs and squeezed but to no avail. She was alone with the darkness. The only light in the room projected in the shape of a wedge from the crack beneath the door. Had it not spoken in two voices—Fafa's and Uncle

Kevin's—the wedge would have been no distraction to Spring-baby at all.

She tossed herself to the side that gave her the best vantage and looked at the only dynamic thing in the room.

"That donkey still down in the pasture?" she heard her uncle ask.

"Spring-baby said something about that donkey," Fafa replied. "I guess it is. I haven't seen it in a while. But you never know."

"Know what?"

"Those people got animals coming and going all the time. I have better things to do than to keep track of them."

"There was a donkey when I was younger. Remember it?"

"Vaguely. I've got other things."

"Yeah," said Kevin. "I used to sneak apples down to him. I'd go down to the pasture almost every day for an hour or so."

"Don't let your mother catch you swiping apples," Fafa warned tepidly.

"Yeah," said Kevin. Then he said, "I saw Spring-baby walk up out of the pasture tonight. Actually, I saw her duck under the barbed wire fence down there. I think she was in the barn. I saw her from the window when it was just about dark."

"Could've been in the barn," said Fafa. "That's where she was when I found her when her mom was on the phone. Chirp Vanhoosen is harmless. That's the boy down there. Mike used to toss the ball with him."

"I tossed the ball with him, too, Dad," returned Kevin. "But I'm not worried about Chirp Vanhoosen. I know he's nice enough. I'm just saying that if there is a donkey in that barn or anywhere else in the pasture, I don't want her going down there. At least not by herself."

"What's wrong with a little ol' donkey?" Fafa said. He sighed tiredly. "So long as it doesn't step on her foot, I don't care if she runs down there to see it. I don't even care if she swipes an apple for it with all that's going on. Your mother. Your mother."

The last words were so soaked with grief that the wedge of light could barely deliver them.

"There are other issues to deal with," Fafa concluded.

Afterwards, the wedge of light was silent but only for a moment.

"That donkey has a name," said Kevin.

"Does it?"

"Amen. Amen for a donkey."

Spring-baby was startled enough to lift her head from the pillow.

"Is that right?" Fafa was receding into himself, pulling his own bare spots inside.

"That donkey's been down there longer than you realize if it's the one I'm thinking of. I used to come up from the pasture around dark myself."

Fafa did not respond; the wedge of light was mute for another moment.

Kevin went on. "I used to have some imagination on me. Used to pretend the donkey spoke to me, made up whole stories from beginning to end. This was when Mike was in the Navy, and Marissa wasn't interested in a smelly donkey anyway, so I was on my own. I had a lot of time to make stuff up. Play around. I grew out of it, but it took some doing. By college I was able to laugh at myself. I had a grip. Right now, I don't know. I guess I saw Spring-baby coming up from the pasture and remembered what a goof I was for pretending the world away. The more I grow older, the more embarrassed I am to think about it."

"We all grow old," Fafa said.

Spring-baby remembered that he was homesick and that he thought everyone went away on an elevator. She lay her head back down onto the pillow and waited for the wedge of light to speak again.

Kevin said, "I know. I know. We all grow old, but when we die, there's Jesus."

"That's what I tell myself."

"It's true," said Kevin. "But with growing up and getting old there comes a time when a person has to look at what he's got, what's right there in front of him. And it's rarely pretty, but we have to deal with it on our own. That's life. Until we meet Jesus, we're nothing but clay just trying to walk it out. I guess that's what I'm trying to say. I see Spring-baby, and I wonder how she'll grow up now that Mike's gone. Will she be able to adjust? This life is hard. There is much too much to handle, and I worry about her. Jesus gives us life, but we have to go through an awfully lot of death to get there. I just think that dreaming up stories only makes it worse. It's like telling a patient a shot won't hurt when it really does a lot more than pinch."

The wedge of light was spent.

"I'm talking a lot. I'm sorry. How's Mom?"

"In the bathroom, I think," replied Fafa. "In the bedroom, perhaps."

The wedge of light retained its tidy yellow glow for a few more seconds before it suddenly relaxed into a shade more tranquil. Then a hinge squeaked, and a door clicked shut. Her uncle's words ricocheted languidly inside her head.

How did Kevin know of Amen? It was a welcome escort into her dream, this question, as she fell asleep.

The beginning of her dream happened like this:

Kevin and Amen were on either side of the fence, though it was her uncle who was on the pasture side. Kevin had on the tie he wore for her dad's funeral, but he was heavier around the middle, stooped: an old man with wisps of gray hair like his father before him. In physical form, the donkey was as Spring-baby remembered him the day she struck him with a rock, yet his comport was different, somehow appealing. About him was an intelligence Spring-baby could only understand with comparison: The donkey held himself the way veteran teachers hold themselves—deliberately, patiently, in harmony with the spinning of the Earth. The two regarded each other wearily as if they had just concluded a long conversation. But when the donkey finally spoke, it was with words plucked fresh from an untouched tree.

"Now you are old, my friend," he began. "You have quite a story of your own to tell."

"My story is bleak. I spent my whole life fighting a battle I cannot win."

"What battle is this?"

"There are no secrets between us, donkey."

Amen made a sound like a straw being pulled in and out of a plastic drink lid.

"I'm sorry your story is as you say it is, but tell me: Will there be a happy ending?"

"There will be an ending, for sure," Kevin replied. "I can only hope it will be a happy one."

"Won't it be?"

"I am a defeated man. I lived my life at odds with my Maker. I could never accept that the devil is smarter than me."

"I'm afraid he is."

Without warning, Kevin clutched the uppermost length of barbed wire and violently pulled it back and forth. The fence posts budged each way with the motion. Amen stood by calmly. Soon drops of blood from the old man's soft hands fell one by one to the weedy divide. "*He-haw! He-haw!*" he yelled with elevating rage. When he finally stopped, he let his arms fall wearily to his sides. His chest was heaving. Thin streams of blood trickled from his wounded palms to the tips of his fingers and dripped away unnoticed. Then slowly, almost timidly, he turned his head and looked one way along the fence. Then he turned his head again and looked the other way. "It goes on and on," he said.

"No, it doesn't," returned the donkey.

And, indeed, it didn't, which is precisely what Spring-baby shared with Chirp Vanhoosen the next day.

XV

Spring-baby told Chirp Vanhoosen all about the conversation she heard; she told him all about the dream, too.

"Prob'ly Amen talked to Kevin, and after that it was me. We din't talk to him the same time, I don't think."

"Uncle Kevin doesn't want me coming down here anymore. He says I'll imagine things that'll hurt me."

"What are you imagining?"

"Stories."

"What stories?"

"I guess the ones you're telling me."

Chirp Vanhoosen appeared as if he were being propped up by the rake he had been using when Spring-baby walked in. He was loosely balancing his extended chin on his hands, which in turn were cupped around the smooth, rounded end of the rake's wooden handle. "I don't fib like that snake," he said, wobbling slightly.

Spring-baby glanced at an open stall: the one in which Chirp Vanhoosen had been working. "I'd like to talk with him myself, though," she said. "Has he been around? Have you seen him?"

"No, but I leave him some food in his bowl like I do every night, and when I get up this morning it wasn't there no more. He must've poofed back again and eat it all up."

"You didn't see him?"

"I seen what he leave me," he said and grinned in the direction of the stall. "He's old and all, but he's got business like everybody else I know."

Spring-baby returned her gaze to the open stall—saw the raked up pile of refuse hay and clumps of manure. "My uncle said the fence went on forever, but it didn't. In my dream, it didn't at all. I remember where it ended. On both sides. It ends where it ends like normal."

"Why did he say it go on forever when it din't?"

"I don't know. I was hoping to talk to Amen. Uncle Kevin said he pretended to talk to Amen, but he knew his name's Amen. So he did talk to him. It wasn't pretend. Amen talked to Uncle Kevin one time, so maybe Amen would know what the part about the fence means. That's what I was hoping."

"Maybe."

"And maybe he could even tell me what the rest of it means. Why was my uncle so mad? And he was old, and there was blood." She rested uncomfortably with the thought then said, "I can't remember anything after that in my dream, and that makes me glad."

Chirp Vanhoosen suddenly steadied himself and eyed Spring-baby proudly. "That part about your uncle and how he really did talk to Amen 'cause he know his name: That's smart."

Spring-baby blushed and smiled a little. "Fafa says I'm like my dad like that."

"I mean, how could he?" Chirp Vanhoosen added. Her smile made him smile, too. "I think you're real smart."

"Thanks," said Spring-baby.

He started back again: his chin, hands, and rake flimsily jointed. "Balaam only *think* he was real smart," he mused. "But what it was was Amen wasn't telling stories at all, but Balaam hit him anyways even though that angel had a sword out as long as the rake I'm holding prob'ly."

Them people I tell you about was Moses's people. They grow like dandelions grow after it rains and the sun comes out. Amen was there right along with them, but one time he got trade off to a man that din't see eye to eye with what them people believe. What I talk about is Balaam. He give advice, which is what he did for a job, and there was somebody that wanted advice for how to get rid of all the people who were like dandelions, there was so many of them.

Remember how I say about the flood and Noah? That was like the rain, and after it come, so did lots and lots of flowers.

Not everybody was happy. What I mean is there was so much yellow that the green got afraid. Green is Moab. That's the people that was afraid to get attack by Moses's people that was yellow.

The bosses of the green need help telling what to do, so they find a man name Balaam. Maybe you hear'd about him in turch. He make believe tons, Amen tell me, which is Balaam tell stories for to get paid, but when he go to sleep and then get up the next day, he tell the bosses the truth: "Go back to your own country, for the Lord has refused to let me go with you."

What the bosses want was to be tell what to do. Also they want Balaam to come back with them and do what is call curse the yellow, which is say bad things about them. But he tell them no, so they go back and think it over. But it din't take long 'cause more of them come back.

It was the same thing that happen one more time—they ask for advice, they sleep, then they all get up—but this time, Balaam tell them, I suppose, I'll go back with you 'cause that's what he hear in the dream he had.

So Amen get saddle up, for he was going, too. He din't even want to go, for what he say was he don't want to see them people in the desert hurt, but Balaam whip his backside and yell, "Get on now, donkey! Get!"

See, Amen figger what it was what tell Balaam to go 'cause he been around, but the mean and nasty way Balaam act make Amen wonder why Balaam was going for *real.* The men that ask him to come had money, so maybe, Amen think, that's why. In the dream it say one way, but Balaam seen it different 'cause that's the way he was.

Amen take a long time for to explain this to me so I could understand it. He tell me he plod along like what he had on was three men, not one.

The first time Amen seen the angel with the sword, he was just standing there in the path. Amen say he glow like the moon in a dark, dark sky: He just stand out, and it make you want to look at him and wonder. Amen, though, he just swerve off the path into a field for to not get too close.

But Balaam say, "What are you doing?! Where are you going?!" then hit Amen so hard it leave a bruise. Amen ain't a dog 'cause dogs yelp, but it was something like that, the sound he make. Balaam hit him again when he din't go back right away, but over and over this time. "On the path!" he tell him, so that's where Amen walk back to, but it was really a kind of limp, and he keep on limping till the smarts wore off.

When Amen, he seen the angel again, this time
there was walls on both sides of the path that make it
so Amen couldn't walk off into the vineyards that was
on the other side of them walls. It was the same sword
and the same glow. Amen, what he did anyways was
walk close to the wall 'cause there was a lot to wonder
about in front of him, and Amen was just a donkey,
even he is a real old one. Then what happen is he crush
Balaam's foot against one of them walls, but he din't
mean to. Balaam got real mad and give Amen tons
more whacks with a stick. "Curse you, donkey!" he yell,
and the words hurt, too, for Amen know they was bad.
Amen tell me the whacks hurt too much, so he din't
just walk off that time, but he done his best.

The angel with the sword wasn't finished. Up
ahead, he stand where Amen and Balaam on top of him
couldn't go right or left but had to stop. Amen, he seen
him with his sword out just standing there on the path,
and when Amen couldn't get by, he just plop down and
wait for to get hit again. And he did. Balaam lay into
him with that stick, but this time it din't hurt 'cause
you know why?

Amen wasn't Amen no more. What I mean is,
something sneak inside Amen, tell Amen to move
aside, please, and go ahead and talk using Amen's
mouth. Amen couldn't explain it good. He just had to
tell me what he hear.

"What have I done to make you beat me these
three times?" say Amen's mouth.

If I was Balaam, I would've been scared, but Balaam
just say, "You have made a fool of me! If I had a sword
in my hand, I would kill you right now!"

But Amen's mouth say, "Am I not your donkey,
which you have always ridden to this day? Have I been
in the habit of doing this to you?"

"No," say Balaam.

And then whatever it was that sneak into Amen sneak back out. Amen shake his head a bit, and when he look up for Balaam, he had to look back down again, for here Balaam was on the ground with his face in the dirt and the angel with the sword was standing over him.

"Why have you beaten your donkey these three times," say the angel, and Amen was glad he sound mad 'cause the bruises still hurt, and he kinda hope Balaam was in trouble. "I have come here to oppose you because your path is a reckless one before me. The donkey saw me and turned away from me these three times. If he had not turned away, I would certainly have killed you by now, but I would have spared him."

Now, Amen never did let on to Balaam like he can talk 'cause he think Balaam—since he think he knows it all anyways—he can just figger it out, what Amen think of him. But when Amen hear that angel say about "killing you" and "sparing him," then Amen say, "I saw what I saw, so now you believe! You beat the one who saved you!" This time it was Amen that talk really, but he let Balaam think it was his mouth again.

Balaam prob'ly din't hear him, though, for he say sorry, sorry, sorry and talk a lot about sin, which is what he tell the angel he did even though Amen just think he was being a jerk that don't see what's in front of him, but what I think, it's the same thing: sin and being a dummy.

Spring-baby waited for him to say more, but when he didn't, she said, "What happened next?"

"They go ahead like before, but this time there was no angel." Chirp Vanhoosen had all but put himself into a trance, wobbling as he did on the rake in a controlled, pensive fashion, barely glancing at the child rapt by his words. "Amen say that Balaam had something to say, but it wasn't curses like what he prob'ly plan before."

"That's why the angel was there: to stop him from cursing."

"Yep, and the angel was gonna use that sword as big prob'ly as my rake. But not on Amen. Amen seen him the whole time, and he would've got spared."

The vision of Amen being battered was sticking to Spring-baby like gum sticks to a shoe. "Balaam didn't have to hit him like he did."

"Don'tcha think I know it!" Chirp Vanhoosen exclaimed, not to be outdone in sympathy. He, too, winced at the vision, tried to wiggle out of the thought. "I feel bad for him, and I tell him so, too, but what Amen tell me right back was, don't. It wasn't him Balaam was hitting, that's what he figgered. Amen was just the closest thing to God that man could get at.

"Why God?" said Spring-baby.

Chirp Vanhoosen shrugged. "Amen really know Balaam. For his job, he make believe like God talk to him. Even high, high ups from all over the land come and give Balaam money for to find out what God tell him. Amen seen it all. He know Balaam like it a real lot when people sit in front of him and listen. Balaam always stand above them. Amen tell me he sound funny like even he pretend another voice.

"What Amen figgered out is Balaam talks but he don't listen. He think he's so smart, smarter than what tell him what to do in those two dreams. Amen think Balaam already know what was in the road with the sword. He just don't wanna believe it 'cause the story din't come from him. So hitting Amen was like saying you're not the boss of me but really who he want to hit was God. He was a stubborn man, that Balaam. Amen ask me why donkeys is called more stubborn, but I don't know why after that."

Chirp Vanhoosen finally grew bored with the rake and set

it aside. When he looked back at Spring-baby, he saw that she was shaking her head.

"I still don't understand," she confessed.

"Donkeys is call more stubborn—"

"No, I mean about the dreams. How did Amen know they were for real this time?"

Chirp Vanhoosen erected himself, sighed, searched his memory with wide, vacant eyes. "I ask him that, too, 'cause that's what I think about them dreams," he said.

"What did he say?"

"Instinct," he soon replied, answering both the girl and himself. "What he has is what we lost, lots of it, and I see what he means. But I been taking care of donkeys and other animals for a real long time."

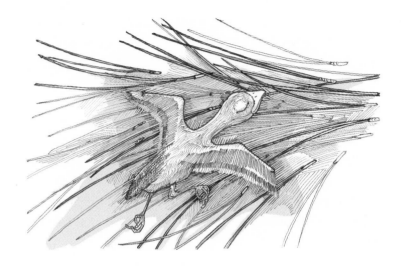

XVI

Spring-baby had once discovered a nestling flailing clumsily beneath a pine tree behind her house. She had whisked it away excitedly and held it before her mother as a cupped offering—the baby bird's neck stretched taut like a Chinese finger trap, triangle mouth gaping, pleading with squeaky, persistent chirps. "Look what I got."

"Oh, no."

"What?"

"Where did you get it? Why did you pick it up?"

Spring-baby was so shaken by her mother's reaction that she was quick to atone: "I'll take it back."

The next day she found the nestling where she had left it: dead, thin wings splayed on pine needle clouds.

"The mother bird didn't want nothing to do with it,"

109

Spring-baby's mother would tell her later. "After you handled it, that is. You should have let it be. The mother must've had a gut feeling that something was off."

Spring-baby had never watered and fed a donkey nor had she ever shoveled manure into a wheelbarrow, but that didn't mean she couldn't understand the certainty of knowing something without ever being told. "I know what instinct is," she asserted and met the eyes of her would-be teacher.

"Amen already know."

"It's a gut feeling. It's something you feel in your gut."

Chirp Vanhoosen nodded. "Instinct." He patted his belly.

"Amen had a gut feeling that Balaam really did know there was an angel with a sword in front of him.

"But Balaam make out like there wasn't for he couldn't explain it, and that make him real stubborn like what I said and prob'ly mad, too."

"Silly."

"Pig-headed. Even that's what you and me is."

"I'm not pig-headed," returned Spring-baby with not a little surprise at the unexpected slight.

"We all is," said Chirp Vanhoosen easily. "When Amen tell me so, too, I got upset 'cause I'm nice, not mean. You won't catch me hitting God. But the way it is, see, is what Amen go on to say, and that's people don't have good memories. They forget real quick, and before you know it, *boom!*—they're right back in a mess of things."

"Forget what?" Spring-baby asked, trying to follow.

"That instinct Amen had: Balaam had it, too. And I do, too, and you, and everybody else in all the world. I hear it call *in-tu-i-tion*, but it's the same as what animals have."

"Intuition?"

"It's what we know without somebody telling us: good and bad, right and wrong, Amen say. The thing is is we all the time forget to pay attention to what we already know. For why?

That's what I say to Amen. He figger we all have two voices when we're born. One's the instinct. The other's been saying you're not my daddy since that fibber give Eve the notion."

Balaam, he get rid of Amen lickety-split, for he don't think swords and angels and donkeys that talk is amusing at all. Amen find himself hauling grain with one owner. Then with the one after that he pull a plow. Every day he seen people act like they don't know the right way, but what Amen say after I ask him, he say they can't help it. It's like when you say to somebody, "Don't look!" What do they do? Amen spend lots of time thinking why don't they listen.

He seen real bad meanness: mean words, mean faces. Ugly what he tell me. People cry when they got sad and yell when they got mad. Sometimes Amen, he seen both at once. And he seen people taking what is not their things, too, and that's bad. People hit him and other animals all the time, and it was sometimes real hard. Even people hit each other. And you know what else, they kill each other tons. And animals, and even some try killing God. Him! But them people that try, Amen say, was brief. Remember about that? Amen is old enough to know. He see lots of people die.

Amen hope Jesse wasn't brief like *that* for he never hit Amen or anybody else at all. Jesse was nice. He buy Amen from a farmer that wasn't.

Them days, Amen din't talk much 'cause he don't have much to say. He done his jobs without a word. Carry what he had to carry. Plow some when it was time. Jesse tell the truth, and that's how he live his life, too, so it was up early in the morning, and bedtime come when only it got dark out, and Amen keep to himself just like he want to think and not make a sound.

When I get up early and come down here in the

way early morning before even it's light out, I understand, for I don't feel like talking to nobody either.

So Amen become like any ol' donkey only still
smart, and you can do both. What I mean is be quiet
and smart, and when he look around at all the people,
it make him think.

I say Amen, he din't speak to people, but I din't
say them people din't speak to him. Jesse had sons, and
one was called David. His job was watching out for
sheep. He talk a lot to them even though they don't
understand, but so to not be lonely in the pasture.

David was a boy. Amen tell me how he was the
youngest.

With them sheep, he make up stories and pretend.
One time he pretend like they're army men, and he's
the high, high up. Or he's the boss in the town, and
they're the people that live there. Maybe another time
something else real funny. And he'd laugh and he'd
laugh, and that make the time pass by.

Amen know this for his ears are big. Remember?
And also David make up other stories, and this time,
Amen's in them.

"I know what you are thinking, donkey, and I can't
say that I am surprised," he like to start out. "Cooped in
a stable. A diet just as plain. You have traveled the land
far and wide and are waiting for just the right moment
to do so again."

That's when he laugh, what Amen say. Then he
pretend how Amen was the king's own donkey that
never had to carry nothing, not even the king's bags,
and how one time he got into one of the king's long
robes, and it was nighttime, and he make believe like he
was the king, and he do it so good, his wife like it, and
she give him a kiss on the mouth. A fat one. Or how
Amen, he one time think he was a person and he eat in
tents and wear clothes like you and me, only old time

ones, and what the people say and how they laugh, and
that make Amen feel bad, but in the end, not really
'cause he seen how them people act, and he figger it's
better to be a donkey anyways.

David come up with all kinds of stories, always
saying "I know what you are thinking, donkey" right
before Amen would do in a story what he really din't do
for real, but Amen din't care at all.

Amen, he begin to look forward to those make
up stories for there's more to life than thinking about
meanness. In the quiet of his work, Amen think
enough to make his head bow low like thoughts is
rainwater, and he's a full up bucket. But when David
come by, it's like he dump it out, and up go Amen's
head to listen.

The rainwater come all the time though. Saul, that
was the real king, he din't tell stories. He fight what
were call the Philistines that keep Amen's bucket full
up with all they done even with his army more small
than the Philistine one.

"I know what you are thinking, donkey," say David
one time. "But do you know what I am thinking?"

What that mean, that mean David just learn from
Samuel he had to go to Saul for to carry his armor
and play the harp, and that's an instrument that make
Saul calm, and David was in the field when he had to
come to his father for to get pick for the job.

"Samuel is a great prophet. I trust his word."

When it come time to go, Jesse give Amen to David
for to ride on, and Amen was happy 'cause he know he
had other chores he was supposed to do far and wide.
He still din't say nothing out loud to David even on the
journey, but that's okay 'cause when you're with somebody
you know real good, you don't always have to talk. That
time, Amen know something with *in-tu-i-tion*. He know
a boy was on his back, Amen tell me. A boy that dumps

buckets out and makes Amen's head lighter.

David, he wasn't shy like what you and me prob'ly would be if we was told to go to Saul. For one time when them Philistines come back for to fight Saul and his little army, David fight Goliath that was a great big man that nobody else want to fight in the valley.

What happen was Goliath say, "Gimme just one of your soldiers to fight, and the both of us will settle it, so the armies won't have to." He keep on saying that for forty days, which is a real long time, but them that was call Israelites was afraid and din't say nothing back.

David, he done stuff for Saul, but he had to take care of the sheep still, and when he come back from doing that to give food to his three older brothers in the army that din't say nothing to Goliath either, he hear Goliath and make up his mind to go ahead and fight him.

"'He's only a lion. He's only a bear,'" is what David tell Saul. It was like David want to protect a flock of sheep. And he din't want to wear the armor what Saul give him either. It din't fit him right, so he just wear what he had on and got some round stones from a creek and put them in a pouch, for what it's for is for his sling. Amen go with him to the valley to watch. He say Goliath's shadow was so big it stretch right across the valley almost to David and that them Israelites prob'ly seen it too and got even more afraid 'cause they din't say nothing about a donkey standing there with them looking on.

"When I was little in my school where I go sometimes," Chirp Vanhoosen said, then paused before he continued, "bigger kids would say things that hurt me and make me scared to go to school anymore. I cry about those things and don't even like to remember them now. Well, Goliath tell David ten times worse. It was about his flesh, which is

your body, and birds of the air and beasts in the field and
how they're gonna eat him up after he's dead. Amen say he
shout them words out in a voice that sound like thunder what
comes before a bad storm."

David, he yell right back, but then Goliath just
run at him. But what happen was David, he sling one
of them rocks from the creek at Goliath, and it hit him
on the head. And even though he's so big, he drop over
like he was make out of manure.

The Israelites yell 'cause they was real, real happy
like you wouldn't believe. The Philistines back away, for
now they don't have their man that can block out the
sun. David, he take Goliath's sword and chop off his
head. Amen turn away for that. But on the way back
to Saul, the sack with the head in it bounce on Amen's
haunches with every step he take.

"He chopped off his head?"

"Even it was big, David had to use both hands for to hold
it up."

Spring-baby let herself imagine rivulets of blood flowing
down David's forearms and dripping generously from his
elbows to the dusty ground as he clutched the head by the
hair. "I would have turned away like Amen," she said with a
noticeable trace of disgust.

"Prob'ly me too," Chirp Vanhoosen agreed.

"But why did he do it at all? That's what I don't get. I'm a
girl, and I couldn't chop off a head."

"But he did."

"And he took it to the king in a sack?"

Chirp Vanhoosen nodded confidently. "Remember he tell

stories that was make up that make Amen forget all what he seen of meanness in the world?"

"About Amen being the king's own donkey and how he got into the king's robes."

"Uh, huh. And you remember about nobody say nothing, not even Saul, and then what Saul want was David for to wear his armor."

"Like Saul wanted David to look like him."

Chirp Vanhoosen smiled as if he were watching someone open a gift he had given. "Saul was a grown-up, and David was just a kid that tell stories, but them stories was the kind that lift heads and what I think hearts, too."

"He beat the bad guy."

"It take a child. Even though Goliath was great big, and he bring death all over, only David can say enough's enough. Amen, he say that prob'ly David know that already when he step into the valley by himself with Goliath."

Spring-baby nodded, but the look of mild confusion remained on her face nevertheless. "But the head. Why did he have to go that far?"

"The head bounce all the way to Saul's like I say, and Amen wonder about it, too."

"So what does he think?"

"Them two voices what I say," began Chirp Vanhoosen with a hint of affected sagacity. "One come from here. The other, here." And from heart to temple, to and fro, his calloused digit tapped the clumsy rhythm of a weighted sack bouncing off a donkey's haunches.

XVII

Kevin sat thinking at the little, round kitchen table. He was alone. A glass and an open bottle of bourbon were before him. Absently, he nibbled his lips as was his habit when lost in thought. He knew where his niece was. Not one apple in the wooden bowl on the table had been disturbed.

He looked at the bowl of apples again. Then leaving his glass to sweat on the table, Kevin bolted from his chair and headed for the pasture.

He was in their midst before Chirp Vanhoosen and Spring-baby could register the slight squeak of the rusted hinges as the barn door was pulled open. "That's alright," Kevin announced.

"Uncle Kevin!"

"Time to head up."

"Why?"

"It's time."

Chirp Vanhoosen shrank into a dimly lit corner of the barn, his head cowed as if he were getting out of the rain.

Spring-baby trailed him with a pointing finger. "I'm just talking with Chirp," she pleaded.

"I know. I want you up at the house. C'mon. Say goodbye."

"But I don't—"

"Now!"

It was the first time her uncle had ever raised his voice to her, and Spring-baby had to take a few seconds to catch her breath, the demand, a shock to her system. "Okay," she mumbled before sulking past her uncle.

Kevin waited for Spring-baby to walk outside and away. Then he returned his eyes to the slumpy man trying in vain to become so much a part of the inside of the barn as to remain unnoticed. "Spring-baby's not allowed down here again."

The inside of the barn did not reply.

"I mean it, Chirp," continued Kevin steely. "I know what you're telling her, and I'm here to say it's not good." He stood for a beat until he was sure he had been heard then turned sharply and made his way to the open door.

"I'm sorry about Mike, for I know he was nice and young almost like me."

Kevin slowed until he stopped altogether but ultimately did not turn back around.

Chirp Vanhoosen shuffled into better view. "It's sad, for I know it is. My mom's at Saint Brigid, too—gone way away— and sometimes I go there to cry."

Kevin inflated ever so slightly then eased the air from his lungs, giving him the look, from Chirp Vanhoosen's point of view, of a small cotton sheet billowed by a gentle breeze. "I know your mom's dead."

"I cry, for I can't see her."

"Mike's dead."

Then Kevin heard the sound that finally made him turn around completely. The laugh stumbled out of Chirp Vanhoosen's mouth like a drunk out of a bar. He contained it with both hands held up tight but continued to snort and snicker anyway. "You know Amen's name what Spring-baby say," he managed to say through convulsions and fingers.

Kevin stood with some intensity, trying to stare the word down. "That old donkey," he said.

"Old, old, old. . . !" Chirp Vanhoosen sang. He started to laugh again but let his mirth fizzle when he noticed he was laughing by himself. "*You* know," he entreated teasingly. He smiled in spite of himself.

"I know what I can put my hands on."

"You know what he tell us both."

"Nonsense," Kevin said, bothered. "He didn't tell me anything. He's an animal. I was an imaginative boy." He paused to look at the simpleton before him, mud-stained boots, ridiculous smile, and all. "Do you even know what imaginative means?"

"Uh, huh."

"You probably can't tell the difference between make-believe and real life," Kevin reflected, shaking his head. He sighed, released some anger. "It's just as well. You seem to be happy. I just don't want you putting fanciful thoughts into Spring-baby's head." He paused. "Fanciful," he said again and continued to shake his head at Chirp Vanhoosen.

"Amen's the one that tells them. He tell me till my ears almost fall off, but they din't 'cause I like to listen."

Kevin grunted his pity.

"Din't you like to listen?" Chirp Vanhoosen asked coyly.

Kevin nibbled his lower lip before he replied. "I heard nothing but braying. That's all there ever was. He. Haw. Believing there was anything else is believing in possibilities that don't exist. I'm a grown man. Growing older every day. And I'm old enough to know that the world is a mean place when it's all said and done. Pretty tales made up in the pasture don't help." He swallowed hard. "Mike was only thirty-three years old. Mom rode back with him from Virginia while Dad and I made the funeral arrangements." Then, arrested by his thoughts, he began to stare blankly through the dark earth at his feet.

"Mike's way away."

Kevin looked up, steadied his gaze. "He's dead."

"No," Chirp Vanhoosen chuckled. "Way a—"

For a spare, bookish man, Kevin was anything but the semblance of pugnacity. Nevertheless, he closed the gap between himself and Chirp Vanhoosen in three brisk strides and struck a blow that made the stable hand twist away from the fist and crumple to the ground with arms raised and quivering.

"It's not funny!" Kevin yelled, spittle flying from his mouth like sparks.

"Don't!"

Immediately, Kevin backed away, aghast at his own realized potential, disgusted with his agitator. "Stupid, stupid man!" he spat. He eyed the door. But he thought better, so he turned and jerked Chirp Vanhoosen up by the arms. "Chirp!" he yelled, his hostility just as suddenly beginning to subside into exasperation.

"For why you hit me in the face like that?"

"Everything's funny to you! I lost my brother! Spring-baby, her father! A son! A friend! His body stopped working! Kidneys shut down! Heart, a piece of lifeless meat! I gripped his hand, and it was cold, ashen, stiff!"

"Way away!" Chirp Vanhoosen insisted, though he hunkered some in trepidation. A hand over which tears now trickled guarded his cheek, tested the new bruise.

"In the dirt!" Kevin heeled the ground beneath him in the heavy way horses do. "A discarded vessel! This," he slapped his chest, patted his legs and arms, "is a vessel! There is no getting around what awaits us all!"

"There isn't. I know."

"We've got just one hope! That's your 'way away!' Until then, we slog it out because what else can we do? We've been sentenced to lives of desperately trying to look the other way! Don't you see? At the end of the day we stare into the cold, ashen, stiff face of what we've been given and pray the hard questions don't come to keep us up at night!" He paused, chest heaving, and gave Chirp Vanhoosen another good look. After a moment, he added with words more tethered, "To be spared that fear. I wish. I wish."

Chirp Vanhoosen kept his distance. He hugged the stall doors as he bumped along, skirting by Kevin and making his way toward the luminescent shard that indicated his way out. Kevin eyed him weakly.

"I shouldn't have hit you," he said.

One leg already out the door, Chirp Vanhoosen stopped and studied the man who also used to throw the football to him. There was a moment when he was mildly transfixed, sorrow curiously tugging at his brows and the corners of his mouth. But soon, his expression relaxed into its dopey norm, and in the end, he shrugged then turned and punched into the sunlight, leaving Kevin to wonder why he had bothered, and when he was through with that thought, why he was still standing in the barn at all.

XVIII

The road had become a thing not of itself, a random direction, a moving image as constant as it was stale. Lorelei had been pressing listlessly into this emptiness for days, sleeping in her car when she got tired, eating what she could buy at gas stations along the way. Her husband was still dead. No butterfly had stolen her way.

"Mike," she'd beckon.

It was in a small town whose name she didn't bother to learn where she finally decided to pull over and let the response, if any, come to her. She was weary of chasing. She let the engine shudder to a halt in front of some main street café shelved between a pharmacy and a bar in the same antiquated brick building. No one was sitting at either of the two dew-covered tables on one side of the entrance. The glow coming

through the broad storefront window was only a little brighter
than the dawning sky.

She stepped into the fresh morning air, passed underneath
a coffee cup-shaped sign, and pushed open the glass-paneled
door on which was etched *Mugs* and its hours of operation. A
young woman on the other side of a counter at the far end of
the café lifted her head from a magazine and said, "Morning"
while a group of three old men slowly swung their gray heads
over to get a look at the stranger who just walked in.

"You serve breakfast?" asked Lorelei.

"Eggs, toast. Sausage or bacon. Pretty basic."

"I'll have coffee, too. Just regular. And over easy on the
eggs. Bacon, I guess. Wheat bread if you got it."

The young woman finished writing on a pad of paper, hit
some keys on the register, and disappeared behind a partition.
Lorelei sat down at the first table she saw. But for the three old
men, she was the only customer.

After a moment, the young woman returned with a mug
and a pot of coffee. "Sugar and cream's on the table," she said,
filling the mug.

Lorelei watched the steam rise, nodded her thanks.

The young woman smiled. Then she returned to her post
and magazine, and from what it appeared, faraway thoughts.

Lorelei took a tentative sip and waited.

The old men resumed their conversation.

"It's everywhere you look, Spurge," said one whose sharp,
blue eyes stood lookout over a crag nose. His spindly body
was like a branch that had lost all of its leaves: a stark
reminder of fuller days. "An epidemic, really. What you and
I call cynicism is what young folks today call wisdom. It's
the TV that's done it, not to mention whatever it is that's
constantly being piped into their ears. Garbage is what I say.
All the time junk." He folded his arms, puffed out his chest
a little.

Next to him, contented, pudgy, and snug in slacks and collared shirt, one of his companions squeezed out a belly-bobbing laugh through his splotchy white beard. "You sound like an old man!

"I am an old man. And you are, too, Deb."

"The topic don't change; the people that talks about it does." There was more laughter from Deb. He even patted the table a couple of times for jovial emphasis.

"You heard me correctly," rejoined Spurge with a calm smile. He pushed his thick-framed spectacles up with a slightly shaky index finger then readjusted the cane he had hooked around his knobby knee. "But I guess I was trying at more than that: the way young ones have become, not just the attitudes they have."

"They have attitudes alright. They bump around like they're the only ones on the planet. It's all about them."

"You can bet I see it, too, Don," said Spurge. "But I saw more of it before I retired when I was still touting the wonders of chemistry to group after group of teenagers. Bumping around. That's how it was alright. Like aimless atoms. In fact, by the time I did finally decide to hang up the lab coat, I was talking to myself mostly. In class, it was only when I made something flash that I got anybody's attention. But when the flashes stopped, why, there's me again listening to myself go on. Now, when I walk, I feel the ground beneath me. I didn't expect everyone to always wonder why something flashed. Not everyone burns for science. But I at least wanted to see them burn for something. But I hardly saw anything. Especially toward the end. Just smoking wicks: minds that were snuffed out, really."

"That's how they are, Spurge. Snuffed."

"I retired years ago, but it still makes me sad."

Deb waved his hand in the air, trying to get the young woman behind the counter to look up from her magazine.

When she finally did, he motioned to her for more coffee.

A moment passed. Then Spurge rubbed his nose thoughtfully. "I had this one kid: bright, went on to college, did well for himself eventually." Spurge finished off the coffee in his mug and shook his head at the young woman poised over him with the pot. "He's the one who lived by himself after his mother passed. The father was gone long ago. Only child. You know the one."

Deb and Don nodded that they did.

"The whole of winter in a house as lonely-looking as it was big. And big it was. We all felt bad for the boy. House got torn down after he sold it and went off to school. But here's what he said in class one day. 'Mr. Witherow,' he said. 'I can prove the existence of the soul.'

"'You can?' I said.

"'Yes. I know the dirt isn't the end of it.'

"Now, I know it isn't either, but with politics being what they are, I had to keep some beliefs to myself. So I just said, 'Go on.'

"'Matter and energy cannot be created or destroyed but can only change its form,' he goes. 'It's a fact, a law. We read about it in this class. The law of conservation of matter and energy.'

"'I remember,' I said.

"'The total quantity of matter and energy in the universe is fixed, never any more, never any less.'

"'Yes,' I said.

"'You know about my mother?'

"I said I did.

"'The body in the casket is matter. It will change form. But it was never just the body that smiled at me, cared for me, told me she loved me.'

"At that point, the boy stopped, seemed to look at his hands folded on the desk. I waited. So did the class. He took one deep breath and went on.

"'What did all those things like I said: that's the energy, that's the soul. My mother isn't dead. She's changed. That's all. What's fixed can never die. In fact, death: What is it but changing? And we do that every day.'

"'True,' I said.

"'People feel sorry for me,' he goes on.

"I told him how sorry we were. It's an awfully big house. The winter's around here are long.

"Then you wouldn't believe it, but he just smiles just as pleasant as can be and said, 'I'm as alone as I ever was,' and that's the last I heard about it.

"How about that," said Deb.

Don leaned back, the two front legs of his chair edging up from the tiled floor. "It might not be cynicism, but is that really wisdom? It's not like he could see her. Loneliness has a way of telling lies. My wife's been gone five years now. I know."

"Mine misplaces names like I misplace socks. Sundowners is what we used to call it," said Deb. He lifted his mug but thought again and returned it to the table.

Spurge absently rocked his empty mug on its sharp circular base. "We're given each according to our needs," he said. "For that boy, it was a different understanding of a basic universal law: a bit of knowledge I threw out not expecting it to stick." His chapped lips spread into a satisfied grin. "I don't know what it is for you, but my feeling is that we're all given something only it doesn't always look the same."

"What something?" said Don.

Lorelei heard genuine confusion, not contempt, in his voice.

Spurge continued, "You asked if it was wisdom and the answer's no. But what it was was," he looked up, twisted his face, ". . . a discovery. That's what I believe."

"A discovery, huh?"

"All he did was open his eyes a little wider."

Don humphed his disbelief. "That ain't a discovery. That's imagination, a nice thought."

"You don't believe in the existence of a soul?"

"I'm not saying that. I just don't think we're equipped to prove it. It's faith is what we need."

"Sure, sure," Spurge agreed. "But everyone needs a Gadly Plain."

"Criminy, Spurge!" Deb laughed. "What's this now? It's sundowners, not sunuppers!"

"I know what I'm saying. It's called Gadly Plain."

"Gadly Plain, is it? Criminy's right." Don laughed a little, too.

"That boy I told you about went on to college. Became a chemistry professor. Burned for it, see. Everyone has their own way of bearing the load we're all given. You have yours. I have my way now. But when I was a kid too young to even imagine the old man I'd become, I had another way, and that was Gadly Plain."

Lorelei didn't notice the plate being set in front of her or the rise in pitch from her cup as coffee was poured into it.

Spurge allowed himself to smile some with the two other men. "No kid wants to hear about God and His mysterious ways. They haven't the patience nor the ability. My friend, Albert, was seven like I was. He died in his mother's arms on the way to the hospital. Aneurysm, I think it was. Poor child. Poor mother.

"'Where did he go?' I asked.

"'Gadly Plain,' I was told.

"'Where's that?'

"'Away.'

"'Away where?'

"'To the great big bigness between when you go to bed and when you wake up.'

Spurge looked up, eyed the men moistly. "That made sense

to me. There was no mystery in that."

Don smiled pleasantly. "I'm glad there wasn't," he said. Then he lifted himself noisily out of his seat. "That's enough coffee for me."

"We each have our own," Spurge repeated.

"That's a nice story," said Deb, joining Don on his feet and chuckling some. "Old men swapping stories is what we are." Then, awkwardly, he pulled out his wallet from his back pocket and took the bill from Don. "Hey, Don. I'll get it today. You got it last time."

"I won't argue."

Spurge finally looked over at Lorelei. "I've never seen you in here before." He smiled.

"I've never been here before. I'm just passing through. I saw the sign." She cut up some egg with her fork.

"You're all by yourself," Spurge observed.

Lorelei returned his smile.

The remaining old man unhooked the cane from his knee, positioned its heel on the floor, and steadied himself up, his back never quite becoming fully erect. Then slowly but determinedly, he shuffled over to where Lorelei was sitting and reached deep into his pants pocket. "It's butterscotch," he said as he pulled out his hand and unfolded his bony fingers. "I used to gobble them up when I was young. I don't as much these days, but every now and then…" His smile widened into something toothier, "Go on. Take it."

She plucked the candy from his soft palm. "Thank you," she said.

"It's not as bad as it seems."

And with that, the old man carefully made his way out of the café, leaving Lorelei, ultimately, alone with God, for the girl who was behind the counter was no longer there, having abandoned her magazine for the short order cook in the back.

XIX

Another train left Spring-baby feeling more abandoned than she already was. It had punctured the sweltering late morning and rumbled away, busily trying to get somewhere else just minutes after she heeded her uncle's order. Spring-baby had waited for the caboose, hoping it might resemble something out of a storybook, but what she discovered instead was nothing more than an empty, rust-covered car, doors open on each side, brief and unimpressive.

So she plodded up the small slope and into the open garage. Granny was standing next to her car, sunglasses already on though the sun's glare was conspicuously absent.

"I gotta run errands," she said dully. "You can come on if you want to. Fafa's down at the office."

"Okay," said Spring-baby. She got in up front, clicked

129

herself in to the fresh-smelling, cloth seat of Granny's Buick. "Where we have to go?"

"Aunt Boo's. Mamau's. Here and there along the way."

"Uncle Kevin came down to the barn."

Granny steered rigidly, replied rigidly, "Coming and going: the animals down there."

And by Granny's terseness, Spring-baby understood, so she remained a presence in the car and nothing more.

Granny left the car running with Spring-baby in it at the post office, but when they swung over to Piggly Wiggly, Granny offered a simple, "Coming?" before she turned off the engine and opened the door. Spring-baby followed her in obediently, shadowed her as she walked up and down each aisle, mechanically loading the metal cart with sundry items. "Mamau and Aunt Boo are getting old," she said.

"Yeah," was all Spring-baby could think to reply.

After they checked out, it was an uneventful ten-minute drive on residential streets to Mamau's: a plain, boxy, brick house her husband bought when the neighborhood was still all white.

"I'm just going to run this in," said Granny as she shifted into neutral. She snatched a brown paper bag from the back seat then hurried up the walkway and entered the house through the front door.

Spring-baby had just started to play with the radio dial when Granny slid back into the driver's seat and backed the car out of the narrow driveway. She did not reattach her seatbelt. "The two of them alone," she said, "it's a wonder why they don't just live together."

Fifteen minutes more got them to a tall apartment complex where everyone who went in and out of the front double door had the look, from Spring-baby's point of view, of giant snails: humped-backed crawlers condemned to a timetable out of pace with the rest of the world. This time, Granny didn't bother to explain. She simply grabbed the other brown paper bag and disappeared for five minutes.

Spring-baby turned the volume down so that it was on complete silence as soon as she saw Granny return and clutch the door handle. "We done?" she hesitated.

Granny hummed a quick, tired reply.

Saint Brigid's cemetery was flung, as many cemeteries are, on the outskirts of town: out of sight and mind but accessible should one want to meditate in the clear silence of inevitability. Bordering the cemetery nearest the road was a line of manicured poplars spaced apart equidistant, and though there was no fence around the gravestones, which were draped over a block of uneven land, a cold welcome was offered by an open gate with overarching latticework under which began the thin drive that meandered through and around the grounds. In the center presided a marble statue of Jesus hanging soggily from a cross. Around the base was a congregation of mute, impassive shrubs. Granny guided the Buick past the lone sentry, deeper into his charge, until she stopped along a part of the drive now familiar to Spring-baby.

"The rainstorm we had probably drenched all those flowers," she said after turning off the engine and waiting a moment. "Most will get thrown into the woods. It'll take a while for grass to grow over the spot." She got out of the car without another word, and Spring-baby followed her lead unsurely.

It was true what Granny had said about the flowers. Roses, their prickly stems having turned pale green, had begun to meld with the dirt. Wreaths of forget-me-nots, daisies, goldenrods, and Queen Anne's lace bearing ribbons cheaply embroidered with "Father" and "Son" lay neglected around and on the mound. Spring-baby noticed a copper-colored marker at the foot of the mound on which was inscribed her dad's name, U.S. Navy, HM2, and two dates.

"What's HM2?" Spring-baby asked.

"His job. He was a corpsman. That's what that is."

The vertical stone at the other end of the mound read "Westbay."

"Your name is on it," said Spring-baby. "And so is Fafa's. Dad's on there, too."

"We bought this plot before you were born." Granny lifted a wreath from the ground then let it fall. "It isn't right to bury your child."

"I miss my dad," said Spring-baby, her eyes beginning to well.

Granny took a deep but fragile breath.

The two stared blankly at the ground.

"Granny," Spring-baby whispered finally. "How come he got so sick?"

"The question keeps me up at night," she croaked. "I don't know. I've begged for an answer."

Spring-baby watched as Granny again reached down to lift or perhaps just touch another wreath. But when her quivering fingertips alighted on the first lackluster petal, she folded to the ground, clutched at the heap, and sobbed uncontrollably into the dirt.

"Oh, Mike!"

Spring-baby's face burned with tears, too, now. She looked helplessly at Granny, lying in the dirt, choking on her immeasurable sorrow. When Granny's wail subsided into something resembling a low, doleful moan, Spring-baby spoke the only words that emerged from the internal flood of her own grief: "There, there. There, there." It had been what the old women had said to her as she wept at the funeral.

"I want him back."

"Me, too, Granny."

"My baby boy."

"I'm so sad."

"I know. God, I know." She slowly pushed herself up from the mound, bits of leaf and dirt stuck to her face, then turned and regarded her granddaughter as if for the first time in a long while. "Your daddy loved you so much."

"I know. I loved him, too."

"You're such a good little girl."

Spring-baby sniffed and smiled a little.

"You're daddy was a good little boy," Granny continued. "Even when he was just teeny tiny he gave me no trouble. When I had to tidy up or cook or whatever I had to do, I would just lay him down in his crib. I'd come back, and do you know what he'd be doing? *'Abba abba abba,'* he'd be saying as happy as can be. *'Abba abba,'* he'd say." She finally brushed off her face, self-consciously fingered the tears out of the corners of her eyes. "Your daddy suffered. And I, his mother, suffered with him. Still do. Will always. He came from my body. I watched him grow. It isn't right that I watched him die."

Minutes passed before Granny spoke again.

"Fafa should be back from the office. He'll be hungry. Are you hungry?"

"A little."

"Let Granny fix you something good then."

She hoisted herself up, locking her bones back into place, then the two trudged back to the car and followed the windy drive past the other side of the statue of Jesus on the cross and out of the cemetery.

On the drive back, there were spare words between them. Fafa was sitting quietly at the kitchen table, bushed and still in his dress shirt and tie, when they walked in from the garage.

"Marissa called," was all he said before lumbering up from the chair and vanishing into the sitting room.

Granny immediately started to warm up a lasagna some-body had left at the house. After the three had eaten, Spring-baby helped Granny clean up. Not a word was said about

Kevin. His car had not been in the driveway when Spring-baby and Granny returned.

It was after dark, after she had clicked off the television she wasn't really watching anyway and crawled into bed, when Granny's pleas began to ricochet inside Spring-baby's mind, churning up riddles she couldn't solve, stubbornly keeping her from drifting off to sleep.

Granny wanted her son to be returned. She wanted an explanation for why he was ripped away. It was Granny's bold defiance of finality that perplexed Spring-baby so, for Granny, after all, was old enough to be in the black and white photographs Spring-baby had seen in little metal frames set atop the doilies that seemed to adorn every end table in the house.

In the darkness of her aunt's one-time bedroom, Spring-baby locked eyes with an impossibility. At twelve years old, she simply could not fathom the innumerable tender complexities of motherhood nor could she even pretend to understand what it would be like to reach for someone, a child born of her body, no longer there. If she were a peach, she'd be whole, blissfully ignorant of the feeling of being pitted. But she was only a little girl whose father was also a son, and only age and maturity held the potential for her to be able to appreciate the difference.

Still, what Spring-baby lacked in years earned and wisdom acquired she made up for in youthful curiosity and imagination. And what she had in these areas trumped by virtue of their combined potency any memory of the wind being shouted out of her.

So her mind became set before sleep finally took her. Earlier in the day, Granny had said she was a good girl. But tomorrow, Spring-baby promised herself, she was determined to be bad.

XX

Misbehavior came early. Before Granny had time to make the morning coffee, Spring-baby was up and down at the barn, waiting for Chirp Vanhoosen to appear while mourning doves cooed back and forth on unseen boughs in the very tree in whose crook Spring-baby had spent many an hour. The sun flamed across the sky. A tiny handful of stars remained toward the horizon not yet reached.

Spring-baby did not know why her uncle had evicted her from the barn the previous day. She was mystified by his outburst, rattled by his urgency, but it did not take an explanation for her to know that her return to the barn was an act of disobedience—an act, perhaps, that would engender a harsher response were her uncle to happen upon her standing there now.

She could grasp an understanding of the consequences but not the reasons behind them. However the thoughts of another outburst frightened her, though, the desire to hear the accounts of a donkey somehow immune from the fate that took her father, her Granny's son, was just too strong.

She was crouching with her back against the coarse, wooden planks of the sides of the barn when she spied Chirp Vanhoosen striding gracelessly over the clumpy pasture ground down to the barn.

He approached her cautiously. "Your uncle tell me, no, you can't come here no more."

"Why?"

"He hit me, too."

"What?"

"He talk about the dirt. He tell me about the dirt."

"Why did he hit you? Why can't I come down here anymore?"

"Afraid."

"Afraid?"

"I think he is. I think it's okay."

"He hit you? Where?"

Chirp Vanhoosen stuck out his left cheek, a purplish bruise smeared across it.

"I don't understand."

"He don't like Amen is what I figger."

"What did he say?"

"Amen's an old animal is all. And kids make up like nobody dies. He even say way away don't exist, but I tell him, no, it does."

Spring-baby cocked her head. "Way away?"

"He hurt my cheek," Chirp Vanhoosen said with a growing smile. "He could have hit the other for all I care."

The way Amen describe it to me was the world was like what happens when you stand on a bridge and drop a stick into a creek that's racing real fast below. The world float farther away. Got lost. Them people Amen was with, the Israelites—they live with the lights out. That's what he tell me. He was there all along when the lights grow dimmer and dimmer. And he say they din't even seem to know what to do about it and only got upset, they were too far down the creek. But he did what he had to do anyway: carry, pull. And there was great big fights. And lots of people got hurt and even kilt. And nobody even notice that Amen had always been around even he was there when David—he was that boy that chop off the head—become king of them all.

Amen, he forget that there ever was a light it was so gloomy. He just walk on like the rest of them—head down, mostly. He and them only look up to curse the rain clouds, is what Amen say. This was the day-to-day of it. Even so many people hit him so much it become normal. Violence is what people do when they're afraid. It's what people do when they're bored, too. Fear and boredom.

Amen tell me lots about Babylonians and how they fight and beat the Israelites, but this time it was Romans that make the Israelites this way. Afraid and bored, I mean. Them Romans are the ones that rub their faces in it, which is the loss they feel. They march around like bullies for they really was. Amen din't talk much then 'cause there wasn't much good to talk about, and anyways, why would he want to, for them all was mean to him?

He was just a dirty donkey. But to some, he wasn't that dirty at all.

You remember that water drop from long, long time ago what I tell you about? The one in the ark? It talk to Amen then, but what he hear now din't come from a drop. It come from a breeze that blow the sadness off of him and out the open door.

"Donkey," it say. Then another breeze come. "The good grass will stretch before you."

"I am tied to a post," say Amen. "I kick the ground at my feet, and I kick up dust and pebbles."

"It will be well for you."

"It was not so after I stepped off the boat."

A couple more breezes come, but Amen hear nothing. Then he hear, "Do you not trust me?"

"I remember because your voice is the voice of a child."

"I am the voice of all that is good."

"I know who you are. You reassure me."

Reassure means make to feel better, for I ask him.

Amen wait to hear more. And he tell me he did. The voice in the breeze say, "Walk with me."

"I am tethered again."

But when Amen look down, you know what, he wasn't tie there no more. The rope was on the ground. He walk away from the post, and he was nudge by the breeze at his back. Amen tell me he walk all night with that breeze, on and on till the sun come up. The voice in the breeze had lots to say and that was how Amen would help out to see death go. For really real. Amen was a good donkey, it tell him. He walk a long ways, out of where the good grass stretch before him, and it was time to head back.

"How?" Amen ask.

"On a back that never knew death."

Amen said he know what that mean, and I know what it mean, too, he din't have to tell me.

There was one great big blow that messed up his

mane then Amen din't hear the voice in the breeze no more. He was alone in the wilderness. The sun was out prob'ly like what it is now.

By then, Spring-baby had stood up and followed Chirp Vanhoosen into the barn, out of sight of the house. She was careful to stay out of the way while he busied himself with the morning chores.

"What would?" asked Spring-baby.

"What would what?"

"Be on his back. Amen already pulled and carried for the longest time. I don't understand why he'd have to do any more. It wasn't his fault. He didn't listen to the fibber way back when."

Chirp Vanhoosen set down the wheelbarrow he was aiming at the open door in order to consider Spring-baby's thoughts. "I din't ask him that. No, not that one."

"It just doesn't seem fair," Spring-baby added. She could see Chirp Vanhoosen rifling through his memory.

"Fair had nothing to do with it," he said finally then lifted the wheelbarrow by the handles again. "Listen and you'll see why."

She followed him back up the pasture and did as she was told.

XXI

A donkey that's alone in the wilderness isn't alone for long. Now there was more people around—remember, like dandelions, but a great big bunch—and it was not like before when he just start out.

Amen, he seen people watching their flocks of sheep, and he seen just travelers, too, and other men with donkeys like him, only the ones that die, walking along paths. Amen hide out behind bushes and trees and hills for he din't want to get tie up and hit ever again and, what really it was, he din't feel right about coming out into the open for just anybody.

But him feeling scared come to an end one day when he seen a man sitting alone on a rock. Amen tell

me the man had his head in his hands, and he was
talking, and this is what he said:

"She has been found to be with child. Yet it is not
because I knew her. Not me. But who? Will I even be
given the courtesy of an answer?"

Then what happen is he take his hands away from
his face, and Amen could see he was crying.

"I am known to be a good man, a righteous man," he
say, "but I confess aloud that I am really a weak man. This
righteousness of which people speak: it is something not
given, not born with, but reached for. When I was told
she was with child, my arms hung limp. They hang limp
now. I fear I lack the willpower to turn my face away
from the wrong that's been done to me."

The man talk on like that till the sun go down and
even in his sleep, he mumble his regrets. That's how
Amen tell me: mumble his regrets.

Amen watch him all night long. Mostly, the man
roll around in his sleep and keep'd on mumbling. But
there come a time when he all the sudden stop and
sleep like a baby even on the ground that was hard
and rocky.

The next day when the man wake up, the first thing
he said was, "I will." Then what happen next make
Amen surprised and even me when I hear it. The man
stand up, brush off his clothes, and call out.

"You are to join me, donkey!"

And when Amen step out from where he hide, that
man, do you know what he did, he laugh like he was
glad Amen was around for to hear what he just say.

Amen return to the village side by side with the
man, and the man din't put no rope around his neck
at all.

What Amen hear when they got there was,
"Joseph! Joseph! Where have you been?"

"Gone to bring a donkey," Joseph say, "and my

pledge to take Mary as my wife."

"You are a righteous man!"

"By the grace of God alone."

Amen, he was happy to be with Joseph and them. Sure, Joseph put things on Amen to carry, and he even had him pull a plow or two, but Amen done it all because he want to and not because he was make to.

The whole time Amen and everybody else watch as Mary's tummy blow up like a heavy balloon till it start sagging some below her waist, which is why she put her hands on the low part of her back like what's call a brace. And her face glow, too. But not really glow. What I mean is she was happy a baby was in that balloon, and you can see it every time you look at her.

Amen, he look at her for a long time when he could. When I ask him how come, he tell me 'cause he never seen a pregnant woman that moves and talks like she's the great big sky and in her tummy is the brightest star. That's how Mary was, he say. Even though she was really a *girl*, Amen even say, he look at her like she was *his* mother, too, and you know Amen never had one of those for I tell you so.

Amen, he was happy for to be with Mary, too. And that's how they was for a good bit of time.

Now, I din't know what a census is, but Amen tell me all about it. It's where they count you up to find out how many you are. That's what a census is. Joseph and Mary had to go to be count like everybody else.

When Joseph got all their stuff together like blankets and food and whatnot for where they had to go to, finally he put Mary on Amen's back.

She was on his back, and she was pregnant. Amen tell me he look back and seen the sandals on her feet and her robe that come to her ankles. Amen had take many people on his back—some real, real heavy and some skinny like me—but he always know somebody

was on top of him 'cause even if they was real light,
Amen sometimes was just tired of walking around with
someone on his back. But with Mary—bulging from
the tummy like she was—Amen feel hardly nothing at
all. What he say was he *want* to carry her, and he din't
care where, for it was more fun than ever before, and
that's the best way he could describe it.

I ask Amen for why he feel like that, and he say
to me that in her tummy was the brightest star, but
with her on his back, Amen got to twinkle some, too.
Amen say he wait a long time for that. Have you ever
wait your whole life to shine just a little, just a smidgen
in the darkness? That's what he ask me. I din't say
nothing, then he say, "I waited hundreds." Then he say
nothing more about that.

The one for real in the sky stand out big and shiny.
I know you know the star I'm saying about. It's from
the story we both know. I know it good. I listen in
turch. But I never know it like how it comes from a
donkey.

They walk a long ways, Amen tell me. He was
fine with it for he got to twinkle. But Mary, she was
groaning like something hurt, and Amen, when he look
around to see for why, his side was wet, and it wasn't
raining; he smell blood, and he know it come from
under her robe.

Joseph, he seen it, too. So he try to calm down
Mary, and say, "Come on, donkey!" but not mean, and
they hurry as best they could to the little town like you
know of. When they got there, Joseph take Mary off of
Amen real gentle, and she sit down while Joseph pound
on doors, but everyone tell him "No."

Amen, he say Mary hold her tummy and groan
even more, and when Joseph seen her, he run harder,
pound harder, ask at the top of his lungs.

Not too far off, what Amen seen, was the stable. I

think it was like a barn with walls and doors like this one, but Amen tell me really it was only a roof hold up by poles. He seen sheep inside. And when they look up and seen him, they say, "*Baa, baa.*"

But one all the sudden go, "Come! Come!"

Amen just look, but he hear, "Come! Come!" again.

When he walk over, a sheep say, "We've heard of you."

"Me?" say Amen.

"Yes, yes. On the back of a humble donkey He will come."

"The baby she carries."

"The good grass will come!" shout one sheep.

"The good water!" shout another.

Then they all start in, what Amen say.

"The good pasture!"

"The sunny sky!"

"No ropes to tie me down!"

And not only the sheep call out but there was a big, hulky ox there, too, that had horns that curve, and he was the one that say, "No lashes ever again!"

Amen turn around and seen Joseph helping Mary over to where they was, but just before they got there and could prob'ly hear, one sheep say, "It will be well for all of us," and it was just like what the breeze tell him, so Amen believe prob'ly they *did* hear of him.

Joseph, he did his best. He throw down a blanket for to have Mary lay down on it. The sheep move away only a little, and Amen did only a little, too, 'cause instinct tell them, Look! Look!

Mary was on her back. She was panting, and Joseph was with her. He hold her hand, then he sit down by her feet and look at where the wet come from. Amen say Joseph, he was smiling, and tears fall on his beard, too. Mary struggle. She yell some and grunt. Amen say he keep on looking down with the sheep and the ox. They couldn't turn away. Amen tell me it was like looking at the prettiest of dawns after the ugliest of nights.

No one go *baa*. Not even the ox, he din't low. When the baby first cry out, it wasn't like a cry like prob'ly you and me did when we come out of our moms. Amen never hear nothing like it. He say the cry start out small but soon build and build and when it did, Amen say his heart beat more and more hard like never before. He had to *he-haw*, he say. And so did the sheep. They *baa*'d. And the ox low real loud.

Joseph, he make his own sound, Amen say, something between crying and laughing hard. Mary did the same but not as much for she was tired out. The baby go on crying.

Amen, when he tell me all this, you should've seen how he got excited about all what he seen. I know the story good from turch, but I never seen how it looks in the eyes of a donkey when he has tears.

"Then the shepherds came," said Spring-baby. "And the three wise men came, too."

"The Magi, Amen say."

"They had the presents and the camels, and they followed the star to get there," said Spring-baby. She absently gripped and released one handle of the wheelbarrow while Chirp Vanhoosen scavenged a nearby corner of the pasture for large rocks that had evidently been dug up, for nearby were fresh posts holding taut lengths of barbed wire untouched by rust. The two were further into the pasture up toward Chirp Vanhoosen's dirty white house.

"Yes, and when they got there, the camels make sounds, too. Some like a deep moan, Amen say, but it was happy."

"Everyone was happy," Spring-baby added.

"A good thing take place."

"Amen got to help."

Chirp Vanhoosen tossed another rock into the wheelbarrow. The rock, flat and dirty, landed with a loud boom.

"My dad still died," said Spring-baby.

"My mom go way away. She's at Saint Brigid, too."

"You said Amen was going to watch death go away. It didn't. Everyone was happy for no reason."

"He watch Jesus be born."

"I know the story, but I don't think it worked. My dad is dead. My dad was Granny's son."

Chirp Vanhoosen lifted a particularly unwieldy rock into the wheelbarrow and pushed it to the center for balance. "They run away to Egypt 'cause babies was being kilt. Jesus come, but death din't go away just when He did. Amen tell me all this. There was a king name Herod that think he only was the king. He din't believe what he was tell about Jesus. Then it weren't well for the babies. It weren't well for the sheep and the ox, for Amen say he keep on seeing them get lash."

"Death didn't go anywhere then."

"Amen think what you say and me, too, for I ask him. But did you know death weren't supposed to go just yet?"

"Why not? The breeze said that Amen would help."

"What that baby come to take away, He need for to help him do it."

"I don't understand. I know the story. I know what happens next. All of it did nothing. Death is still here. Do you remember how your mom looked? I remember how my dad looked. I kissed him. I know death is still here because I tasted it on my lips."

Spring-baby was crying now, a little girl orphaned in a pasture with an imbecile and his stories. Her sorrow repeatedly jolted her small body. She let the tears and snot pour down her face.

Chirp Vanhoosen stood with his arms hanging dumbly by his sides, gaping at the stricken child before him. "Don't cry," he said after her first surge of emotion. He spoke gently, she having become as fragile as a tiny flame struggling against the wind. "You kiss your dad?"

"On the lips," she managed to say. "At the funeral home." Then she wept fiercely.

Chirp Vanhoosen waited patiently. "Nuh uh," he said finally, shaking his head slowly, correctively. "Not what love you, really."

XXII

I tell you about way away," began Chirp Vanhoosen. "You said my uncle didn't believe in it," replied Spring-baby as she drew her forearm across her mouth and nose.

"It's where they're at. It's where they go to."

"My dad? Your mom?"

"Uh huh."

"You said your mom was at Saint Brigid."

Chirp Vanhoosen smiled bashfully. "It's where I go for to talk to her, but Mom, no, she's not there for real."

Spring-baby watched Chirp Vanhoosen place various-sized rocks into the wheelbarrow. Something in how he did it with pleasant abandon provoked her to anger. "You're making it all up!"

Chirp Vanhoosen let fall a rock he had just picked up from the ground. He did not want the girl to be angry with him. He had a sorry look on his face. "Amen tell me—"

"A donkey!"

"A donkey that—"

"You've been telling me stories!"

"True ones!"

"I'm not retarded like you are! You lied! I can tell! Death didn't go anywhere! It's like I said!" She shook the wheelbarrow by the handle with all the violence she could muster in her brokenness. "You don't talk to your mom 'cause she's not there!"

"Way away," Chirp Vanhoosen said, hurt. "I do. She is."

Spent, Spring-baby let go of the handle then leaned limply into whatever part of the wheelbarrow would catch her first. "Stories," she repeated weakly. "I don't know what way away is."

"I din't know till Amen help me."

"Is it heaven? Is that it? Why don't you just call it heaven like everybody else?"

Chirp Vanhoosen returned to the rock he had dropped, lifted it with a soft grunt, carried it to the wheelbarrow on which Spring-baby still bounced listlessly. "I look at the most beautiful thing, and you look at it, too, but me and you, we think about it not the same. Neither we talk about it the same, too. And Amen din't say that to me. I think it on my own—even I am retarded."

"My mom go way away for she had cancer. She got sicker and sicker then one day it was her time. My dad say her time come. I think like you. Every day I was sad. I cry. I figger I know why we're here, and that's for to wait for our time and that's all.

"I do my chores. One day I come down to the barn and, here, there's a donkey that I don't know where he come from. I look at him 'cause I din't know, and I only find out when he tell me.

"'Boy,' he say to me. 'Tell me your troubles. I am an old donkey, but my ears are still upright and very large.'

"I tell him about my mom and about my time to come."

"Then he ask me, 'What did your mother teach you about love?'

"I tell him my mom, she say love is the one and only thing that holds us together even when we go way away. It is above everything else. It is as sure as the line that makes a circle.

"'Then the time of which you speak: it is a time like any other. It'll come, and it'll go.'

"I come down to the barn all the time after that, and when I do, I find out my mom know about love good.

"You hear all about what Amen do. How the good grass was take away, and it wasn't his fault. About Adam and Eve, and it *was* them. About Noah and the ark. About Abraham and Isaac and the ram that got kilt. I tell you about Moses and Balaam and David and Joseph and Mary and the sheep that talk and the ox, too, about lashes. Amen had a long life. There is stories I din't tell you. I find him when he poof into the barn. He got to help watch death go away. His back never seen death like I tell you. You say it din't work, and that's wrong. Sad times still come, I learn. But what Amen find out, all them stories I tell you, they was just part of a big, big story that, at the end, it make me happy and you, too, if only you listen to the rest.

"Only one thing can make death go away. I know it's like what my mom and I feel, and it's prob'ly like what you and your dad feel. It's what I can't even talk about for I don't know how. Amen, he say Jesus is as sure as a line in a circle. Amen find that out when he watch Jesus grow up and even after when the people come to him for to find out why about the circle, but they prob'ly din't call it that.

"Amen tell me what he seen and hear about Jesus. You 'member the drop and the breeze? I don't understand all what Amen say, but it was about how love come together and walk like me and you and talk like me and you and everything else, for God, He seen how dark the world got and He din't want to see it dark no more. This was what Jesus was for. Mary carry him in her tummy, and Amen carry them both on his back. Amen, he din't know he take that much weight 'cause he din't even feel it. But he got to watch Jesus, and he got to listen, too. And Jesus look at him like he wasn't surprised at all to see him like he know him all along and even talk to him before. And 'cause Amen was smart, for he live so long, he figger it out who Jesus really is.

"You know the story, I know, for I tell you the other story about the stable where the baby get born, and there was animals. Amen's a good teller."

People weren't the only ones that listen when Jesus talk, even though the animals know a lot without being told. They had *in-tu-i-tion*, what we talk about before. People say animals are dumb. Amen, he say no, it was that people forget real easy and pretend like they was the boss, only they're not.

One time Amen, he seen another donkey that was being hit and hit so much that he *he-haw* for the man with the lash to stop it, it hurt. Amen seen this all the time, and it make him sad 'cause why did the man have to be so mean? Nobody that seen it did nothing. They just walk by, and Amen, he say they din't even look like nothing was happening, and they can't hear the awful *he-haws*. The other donkey go down on his knees, the man hit him so hard, but what Amen seen next, he never seen before.

Jesus come there, and he go right up to the man and say, "Put down your lash!"

The man with the lash, he put it down, but he tell Jesus that he had to get the load the donkey carry to the market to sell or else he will have no way for to provide for his family.

"Not by the lash does fortune come," say Jesus, and what he done next was help up the donkey.

Amen, he tell me that not many people know about this story, but he say it happen 'cause he was there, and he seen it.

Amen, he seen a lot what Jesus done and with them big ears, he hear a lot, too. People come from all around and sit in front of Jesus, and some just stand, but them people all listen real hard, for they like to hear what Jesus tell them.

Amen say it was like they all remember. They remember the feeling of how to be little. It was safe. No worrying. When I was little, I feel safe. Din't you? Prob'ly you did. But I'm older than you, so I know what I feel don't stay around. It don't for nobody is what I figger. We grow up, and we worry, but Jesus tell them, you don't have to do that.

"Listen to me," he say.

They listen, Amen say, for nobody feel safe, and everybody worry themselves to death.

Only the world was still very dark and full up of death when Jesus got born into it. He know it, and he come to do something about it. That stick that go down the stream? He want it back. There was one way to get it, what Amen tell me, and that's why Jesus feel heavy even though he wasn't.

Amen make out like he was a reg'lar ol' donkey even he was older than death, for he want to hear Jesus, too. When the crowds got real big, Amen would stay out of the way and chew on grass and swish his tail. Amen din't know he would get to carry Jesus again and twinkle some more.

He din't figger he would get catch again either, but he did. For there was lots of people with no donkeys, but that's okay 'cause when he was tie up someone say, "There he is. It is a miracle. We were told, and here he is. A donkey never ridden."

Amen din't know why they say that, but he go along with them anyways 'cause he seen them with Jesus, and he wasn't doing nothing else anyways, just waiting for waiting's sake, he tell me, and he din't like being tie up.

The men take Amen to Jesus which make him surprised.

"Hello, friend," Jesus say, and he smile at him and he pat his back. "Your back is good and strong. It has served me well. Let it serve some more."

And then he got on Amen's back, and Amen just start walking, for what he say, he know already where to go, but he din't know how to get there.

He walk up a hill, and into Jerusalem, which is a city where Jesus had to go to. There was people there, and they put down palms for him to walk on, and they say "Hosanna!" and they was happy, and everybody stare and smile, and Amen smile, too, only nobody could tell 'cause he's a donkey, and they don't know.

Everybody knows what happen next in Jerusalem, and I know you do, too. Amen din't see it all though. It's hard to sneak with hooves, he say. But he hear about it. The garden. The kiss. Amen know the cock which is a rooster that crow 'cause he seen him do it, and the cock just say, "It's my chore—a chore like your own."

Amen din't see, but his ears catch it when Jesus cry out, even though he din't really want to hear that. And he hear it when Jesus got yell at when he walk up another hill. He follow the people at a trot after he hear that. He say he din't care if they seen him or say anything nasty. Jesus was love come together. Amen, he want to see how death was gonna go away.

Amen *did* listen before when Jesus tell them, "I am the lamb of God." Amen remember good what Jesus say to them.

Amen know lots of lambs. He din't like to hear them when they find out the knife was for them either.

Amen know what lambs was for. He know why Jesus ride on his back to Jerusalem. To try to make things good for all. Safe. No worrying. Not even about times.

Amen look up at Jesus. Two men were on crosses, too. They all was talking some, Amen say. Then one man got mad, and the other started to cry. Then more and more time pass, and it hurt Amen to watch.

Then Jesus cry out. And the earth shake. When I ask him about that, Amen tell me the sky grow dark, even it was day out.

Then just like before with Noah and his son that grab Amen, someone seen him and say, "A donkey left alone and untethered is a donkey I'll call my own."

The man was rough, but Amen din't try to run away. What he seen happen to Jesus, it make him like he was there but not there. If I seen all what Amen seen, I'd prob'ly be doing some thinking but doing a lot more feeling, really.

"You said they were looking for a donkey that was never ridden," said Spring-baby shrewdly. "Amen was ridden lots. I don't understand."

"I ask Amen about that, too. He say what all he can figger is 'cause he never know death, that's why he wasn't really, real ridden."

"Because he never knew death?"

"That's what he figger."

Spring-baby watched as Chirp Vanhoosen topped off the wheelbarrow with a large stone. Then the two stood for a moment and looked at the work that had been done. Finally, Spring-baby said, "I think I know why."

"Why?"

"Because that's how Jesus first loved him."

"Prob'ly that's it," Chirp Vanhoosen said. He grabbed the handles of the wheelbarrow, bent his knees, and lifted the load with some strain.

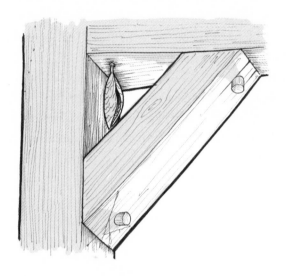

XXIII

Chirp Vanhoosen had drawn a bead on the rust-bitten gate just up from where the repairs to the fence had been made. He moved stiffly, determinedly. Spring-baby was close in tow, and when they reached the gate, she quickly figured out how to lift the metal cuff that held it in place so that she could push the gate open. It swung wide with a whiney screech.

"D'ya know what I wonder?" said Spring-baby as Chirp Vanhoosen struggled past her. "About Amen and how Jesus first loved him?"

"You can tell me," said Chirp Vanhoosen.

"Why did God let it get so far? The stick. Us all."

"What do you mean?"

"He first loved Amen when he was really never ridden.

He loved us all that way, I think. Why did Amen have
to go through all that he did? He never knew death, but
that didn't mean he never had a hard time. I mean, I don't
understand why Amen had to go through all those things
you told me when God knew all along that death would
go away."

"Prob'ly we're not suppose to understand. Like Moses."

"My dad is gone. I never saw Granny cry before, but now I
have. Why did she have to lose her son? Why did my dad have
to go at all if Jesus already beat death with death? They killed
Jesus. Death to take away death, right? It's like what I learned
in school: a double negative makes a positive. Two no's make a
yes. Wasn't that enough?"

"Jesus only beat death when he got up again. Three days
later."

"I know the story. There was a tomb and a great big rock
that was moved away and an angel that said, 'Go away. He's
not here.'"

"Death din't work on Jesus. Not forever."

"It worked on my dad."

"Did your dad know the story like me and you?"

"I guess. I don't know. Probably."

A short distance away from the pasture gate was a small
knot of woods into which poked a walking path well-worn
from frequent travel. Chirp Vanhoosen rolled the wheelbarrow
past where the path ended and did his best to catapult the
rocks into the brush.

"D'ya know that man like I say that catch Amen and
say, 'You're mine?'" He was fishing the heavier, more stubborn
pieces out of the wheelbarrow and heaving them where the
others fell.

"Lots of people threw ropes around him. That's what I
mean. A hard time. It doesn't make sense."

Chirp Vanhoosen leaned in, apparently afraid that even the

bushes and the trees nearby would betray him. "That's exactly what that man say."

From what Amen seen, the world become like a sheet over a lamp. It all was dim out. The people and the animals walk like they had water up to their knees. Amen seen some people take Jesus away, but he din't see nothing else for the man I tell you about catch Amen.

"You're mine now, donkey," he say, putting ropes around his head and neck. "Or should I call you Amen? No, donkey will do just fine."

Now, Amen never say nothing to this man, so how come he know his name? Amen got jerk down the hill, the one where Jesus got kilt.

"You don't have to play coy with me," say the man with an easy smile, and when I ask what "coy" means, Amen just say "shy."

"We shared pasture, me and you," say the man. "You are old, I know, donkey—it is no secret to me—but I was there to see your beginning and the beginnings of many others."

"I don't know you," say Amen.

The man laugh great big. "The world knows me. It is what keeps me fed. It shelters me in times of trouble."

"Who are you? Of what trouble do you speak?"

"Reunions, donkey."

"Reunions?"

The man laugh again. "Thank God for deaf ears." Then he really began to laugh, and it was so much that he had to stop tugging Amen along, put his hands on his knees, and catch his breath.

Amen shake his head. "How can you laugh?" he ask. "Can't you see that the world has grown dark?"

"Yes-s-s-s-s," reply the man as he start again to tug on Amen.

Amen snort.

"You should be used to this darkness by now, donkey," say the man.

"I am used to a long life."

"A long life of darkness. I knew you in the garden. I knew you, too, in the ark and when you put your hooves on dry ground. I know the hopes you had. You have them now, I can tell. These reunions, these glimpses of hope—trouble, all. You agree with me. They make your heart heavy with want.

Amen tell me he never think about it that way and that he did sometimes feel bad, for he *was* tell that it would get better, but every morning when he had to get up and every night when he go to bed, it wasn't better.

"I am a realist," say the man, and that mean he believe in what he can see and touch. "The most famous realist, I suppose. The darkness can be overwhelming, but at least you can trust it. Promises, never mind how wonderful they sound, are still nothing but spoken words: flimsy tokens out of step with what you wake up to.

"You've walked a long ways, donkey. You've carried your hopes like so many other loads. Put them down. You already know how burdensome they are. What I'm offering you is a lighter load. It's one you're used to. Why not find peace where it can be found? You already know it's not to be had in lofty promises."

"But the promise is good."

"The promise can be made of gold, but if you never see it fulfilled, well, then it's nothing more than a carrot dangling from a string on a stick. And you, donkey, of anybody should know about that."

Amen say nobody ever dangle a carrot from a string on a stick in front of him, but he know what the man mean anyways.

"I know this promise-giver," say the man. "He means well, for sure. But I'm not convinced he fully appreciates your needs or the needs of anybody but himself, for that matter. You see, the one thing you need, he greedily withholds, and that's perspective."

"I have perspective."

"You have nothing of the sort. You have suffering, you have confusion, you have fear, and you have hope as unfulfilled as a carrot left to rot on a string."

I ask Amen tons of questions 'cause this man, he use a lot of words I don't know. Amen explain them to me. I can tell that you know about them, so I'll just tell you what happen next.

The man wouldn't stop jerking Amen along.

"Where are you taking me?" ask Amen.

"Does it matter that you know?" say the man with a violent tug. "You've never known before."

"I trusted."

"Trust me."

So Amen plod along behind the man but only 'cause the man had a rope. They walk through the city. They walk far, far into the desert. If the moon come, they din't know. They only know it was morning when the coyotes din't yip or howl no more.

The man walk like he know where he was going, Amen tell me, and he din't even get tired. When the coyotes begin to yip and howl again, Amen say he have to take a break.

"Fine," say the man. "You out of anybody deserve it most."

And that was when Amen know it was the fibber that catch him.

The fibber, he still hold onto the rope, but he sit down and look up at Amen. "Don't you? It wasn't your fault, this darkness-s-s-s. What did you do to deserve this? You just got caught up with it. A donkey, and who cares about that? Right? I've seen how you were treated. I know the paths you've trodden. And so a promise walks right up to you and says, 'I'd like a ride 'cause you're special,' and you're expected to go along with it like years upon years of pain and loss never happened. It doesn't make sense."

"It happened," say Amen.

"Sure it did! Yes!" The fibber got so excited he start to stand a little, but then he sit back down again. "You take your rest. I say so. Do it for yourself and no other."

Amen was happy he got to rest, but he din't like how the fibber keep on twirling the rope.

After a little bit, the fibber say, "I know what I am called. I know how I am known. Your big, aged eyes betray your fear. Do not worry, donkey. You see the world around you. My best weapons now are honesty and truth. You were promised to help death go away. You saw his body come off that cross—how mangled it was, how bloody and lifeless. What do I have to fib about? In the eyes of God, you'll always be a dirty, little donkey. And me? I'll be the guy that always tells it like it is."

"Perspective," say Amen.

The fibber nod. "You won't find a greedy bone in my body."

But Amen say, "You have nothing I need."

"Is that so?"

"It is true what you say about the loads I've carried, the paths I've trodden."

"Heavy, long."

"Not easy."

"Undes-s-s-served."

Amen shake his head some and feel the rope on him, and that make him real afraid, but he say to the fibber anyways, "What business is it of yours that I've walked so long and carried so much?"

"I am in the business of suffering, donkey. The torments I've dealt, the deeds that are within my rights to execute—some souls will walk longer and carry more than you've ever known. But you: What have you done to earn this curse of life without death in a lost and wicked world, a world too stubborn to be anything else?"

"It is no curse I've been given."

"Of course it is! We are both fallen, you and me, doomed to an eternity of pain. Only I know so. I have embraced it. I have come to terms, found perspective. Your Jesus, though, would have you walk forever and never so much as tell you why. I *do* have what you need. Knowledge! Surely you see the comfort to be had in its possession."

Amen tell him again, "You have nothing I need."

The fibber shake his head like he was sad. "Stupid, stubborn animal. It would be so much easier to lay all your hopes aside and acc-c-c-cept what's before that long nose of yours, but no. You'd rather be charmed into believing there's something more, something better."

"Reunions."

"Nonsense."

"You called them times of trouble."

Amen say the fibber stop playing with the rope when he tell him that.

"You are a liar," say Amen.

"I am the only truth there is."

"This is the real nonsense. Can't you see? I am a donkey that talks. I have been walking this earth since before death came."

"I saw your beginning."

"So you know. And you know the truth of other donkeys. The ones that grow old. The ones that die. I am the possibility you fear."

It was the fibber that snort this time, and when he

did, Amen say he seen glowing sparks that shoot out
of his nose. The fibber stand up, too, and wrap the rope
around his hand tight. "I have you in ropes, donkey," he
say. "I led you into the desert where there is no one else
but me. I will see your ending. Your rest is over."

And then the fibber yank hard on the rope and jerk
Amen till it hurt.

"Where are you taking me?" ask Amen.

"Where you've never been."

"Death?"

"Enough talk. I've waited a long time for this."

But then Amen, he notice there was no more yips
or howls neither. And it had got lighter, for what it was
was the sun coming up. The fibber pull and pull, and
Amen straight his legs 'cause he din't want to go, but
Amen feel the pulls getting more and more weak like it
was the sunlight that done it. Then the fibber, he pull
so much, but Amen feel like he wasn't doing it at all.
The light was really, real out. The fibber sit down in
the dirt, and he was so mad, he din't even look at the
rope no more. Amen wait, but the fibber, he din't move.
Then all the sudden the fibber snort like before with
the glowing sparks out of his nose, and there was so
many sparks it cover his body like he was all sparks,
and when they go out, the fibber, he wasn't there sitting
on the ground.

Amen think he's alone, and he din't see nothing
at first, but then he feel hands pat him, and he feel
hands take off the rope from his body, and when they
throw away the rope he finally did see the hands. Amen
tell me he never seen hands like them before. I ask
him what he mean by that. He say that if he was the
possibility, then the hands with holes right through
them, they was the proof.

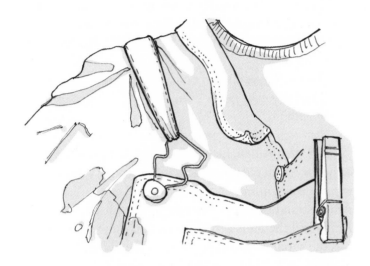

XXIV

Y ou've told me nothing," said Spring-baby sourly after Chirp Vanhoosen dropped the last big rock onto the ground.

"I tell you about how the fibber catch Amen but not for long 'cause Jesus come back for to not let that fibber take him away with a rope and kill him."

"The fibber talked about honesty and truth, about how the world really is."

"That's what he say."

"How is he not right?"

Chirp Vanhoosen rubbed his chin with his wrist. "Amen is possibility."

"I know what that word means. It means could be. It means maybe, perhaps."

"I think I know what perhaps means."

"You can't see it yet."

"Amen seen proof."

"I know the story. I knew it before I ever even heard of Amen. Jesus rises from the dead, and we're all supposed to be real happy, but I don't know why. What the fibber talked about—all that death and suffering—nothing's changed."

"Jesus got up. Amen seen his hands."

"I don't understand!" Spring-baby looked like she wanted to cry, but instead she sniffled hard and gritted her teeth against the in-rushing tide of confusion. "I've never heard Amen speak. When I ask about my dad, I'm given stories. You've been telling me stories ever since my mom left me here. Why? To make me feel better? To let me know that everything's going to be alright?

"I'm going to be in middle school next year. I know something about pain and loss and the world around me. I don't know what these stories are supposed to mean. I don't feel better. I just don't. I feel like I have to guess about why I should feel better. Or, I should just know why and shut up and be grateful. But how can I when there is nothing to fib about? I want to see possibility. I want to see proof. I want to see hands take the ropes off of *me*."

Chirp Vanhoosen was shaking his head slowly, worriedly. "Little girl," he began but could say no more. He just kept shaking his head and looking at Spring-baby with an arresting pity.

"Why is that bad?"

Then Chirp Vanhoosen stopped.

"You never asked?" said Spring-baby, and she could tell by how his eyes searched his thoughts before him and how his jaw slacked some that he hadn't.

"I just believe it," he said eventually.

"Believe in something better?"

"Uh huh."

"Green grass."

"Green grass."

"I wish that was something to me," said Spring-baby. She looked up at Chirp Vanhoosen with the expectation that he shrug away her silly despair and roll the wheelbarrow back into the pasture in clumsy retreat.

But he just stood there as still as the rocks he discarded, his gaze anchored to the earth.

"How is it something to you?"

After a moment, Chirp Vanhoosen pulled his eyes up from the ground.

"I know I'm not smart like you," he stammered. "I was in middle school, too, but only a different one. I know what you ask me. How come I know the grass is green? How come I'm not afraid every day when my mom's still gone, and I see things that people don't think I do? I'm not smart, but I know when I feel sad, and I know when I feel happy, and I know both of them things are inside me and are really real. I see them outside, too, all the time. I see what's sad, and I see what's happy, and they're really real like on the inside. I can't hide from what's sad even if I want to. It's always with me. The sad, it's big. My mom. Your dad. The dark world Amen tell me about."

"It's still dark," Spring-baby interjected.

"I know," said Chirp Vanhoosen. "Everywhere it is, but like what I say, it's not that way only. On the outside it's dark, and sometimes on the inside, too. And it can be big, great big, so big, even when your eyes are really open, it's like they're shut."

"It is big."

"Yes." He looked at the work he had done, then over Spring-baby's head out toward the pasture and the dispersing fog above it. Finally, he looked at the girl. "Before my mom go way away, I didn't think she would do that. Not Mom. Not ever. She did, though. Way away. You said about the green grass. Something better is what it is. It's something to me, for you know why? I cannot think of the green grass either. Not what it prob'ly really is. Like my mom and what happened, I can't."

"Why?"

"I don't know how."

"What do you mean?"

"The good. The other one. It's what else there is. It also is big, great big, so big, but different, for even when your eyes are shut, it's like they're open."

"What's happy?"

Chirp Vanhoosen nodded. "Yes. It means something to me, for it's so good I don't know how to say so."

Spring-baby thought then of her father's eyes—how the powdered lids pulled tightly down over his sunken bulbs in a way that made her father's face look like a grotesque caricature of what it once was. She closed her own eyes and vainly waited for her heart to stop hurting. It didn't, so she opened her eyes and waited for Chirp Vanhoosen to tell her why.

He grinned kindly before he spoke. "You want the ropes take off?"

"I want to see even when my eyes are shut. That's the one I really want."

"Then it's like what I tell you. It's what I figger out."

"Tell me."

"What the dark is: it's bigger than me and you and Amen, too. That's what you hafta know."

"I do know."

"You can't stop it even you want to."

"But the good?"

"That's what can. That's what did. Only."

"How?"

Chirp Vanhoosen's two sharp shoulders raised up like they were being pulled up by strings. "Jesus: He loves."

But Spring-baby gritted her teeth even harder and stomped the ground suddenly with tantrum-like violence. "The stories? They're just stories."

"They happen for real."

She stomped again as if she were trying to drive her heel to the center of the earth. "Where is He!?" she yelled. "There's still bad in the world! Where is He!? Where is He!?"

At first, Chirp Vanhoosen said nothing, did nothing, letting his long arms hang limply at his sides, making no attempt to appear as anything but a gaping dolt. Only his eyelids moved up and down like languid shutters. When once they remained down, Spring-baby imagined she had pushed him too far.

"Chirp," she tried.

And at that, he opened his eyes and slowly drew air into his lungs then let it go with an easy rush. Then his lips came together; his arms came to life. And bit by bit, he gathered himself up until he stood before Spring-baby a man in bloom.

Spring-baby did not try again. She didn't have the time, for in confident strides, Chirp Vanhoosen walked around the wheelbarrow and hugged her to his chest, a rough-looking hand cradling the back of her dirty blonde head not roughly at all.

In her acquiescence, Spring-baby found the peace she needed. It smelled faintly of fabric softener, felt cool against her cheek. Yet she didn't have years enough to experience the epiphany even though her young life was now discolored by death. She simply remained in his embrace, secure and safe, while somewhere other children wailed their displeasure as other parents calmly made rights.

XXV

They worked together the rest of the morning. They worked in glad silence. Spring-baby lifted what rocks she could—from the pasture and from the wheelbarrow to the grass—while Chirp Vanhoosen was quick to snatch up the heavier ones. When they finished, they moved on to other chores, still without a word between them.

The day ripened into a thing as glaringly bright as it was sweltering. Their temples were damp with sweat, and their eyes hurt with squinting against the sun. Spring-baby helped Chirp Vanhoosen collect small fallen branches to throw into a brush pile then she helped him tidy up a corner stall back at the barn. It was for a horse, he said. Spring-baby dumped out stale water from an old plastic bucket and filled it again with a hose.

"When is the horse coming?" Spring-baby asked.

Chirp Vanhoosen shrugged in his usual manner. "I just know he is."

Spring-baby obliged the call from an open door to lunch, but after a lonely meal of a sandwich, chips, and sweet tea, she dashed back to the barn, hoping that Chirp Vanhoosen would still be there. He was walking back down to the barn from the little white house on the hill overlooking the pasture as Spring-baby slid under the barbed wire fence and made her way to the shade of the barn roof.

"I like peanut butter and jelly samwiches," he said when he got within hearing distance. "And Pepsi to wash it down."

"Is this the end?" she asked.

"Of what?"

"Amen got the ropes taken off. Somehow he got to Kentucky, but really the story's over."

"Why?"

"Is it? Or is there more?"

It was easy for Chirp Vanhoosen to see the answer she wanted. Despite the shade of the barn roof bathing her from the chest down, the sun caught her in the face. She waited for an answer with her forearm shielding her eyes.

Amen wasn't leaved alone there in the desert so far from Jerusalem after what Jesus did, take off the ropes. Jesus start walking, and Amen, he follow like it was what he was supposed to do only Jesus din't say so out loud. Amen just know. And it was a good walk, what Amen say, real good, not hard, and when they got to where they was going, Amen wish he could've walk with him more.

They was at the place where John and the others all was, that's what Amen find out later. Jesus tell Amen to wait, and that's what he done. When Jesus go away, and when Amen look down, in front of him was a great big bucket of fresh water and a great big pile of oats

and grass as green as nothing he seen before. He eat
for he was hungry, and when he got done, there Jesus
was again, standing next to him, smiling and patting
him on the back.

"You will go with John," he say.

"He was with you at the cross?"

"Yes," he say, so that's what Amen done.

He was happy for to do it. John, he was kind, and
what Amen did, he take John all around for he had a
lot to say to people. John talk and write, and Amen say
it was like he couldn't do it all fast enough. Amen help
tons. He carry around his things like his blanket and
food. And John, he always treat Amen good.

One time, though, the Romans that were the ones
that put Jesus on the cross, they want John to stop all
he was doing, so they try to kill him in boiling oil. That
was in Rome. And when that din't work, they make
him go far away from everybody, and where it was was
Patmos, which is an island. Amen go, too, 'cause he's
just a donkey is what them Romans say.

John stay in a cave and got real skinny 'cause all
what he eat was locusts that are bugs and honey. His
hair got long and messy just like his beard. Even his
teeth turn black and fall out, but Amen say, he still
smile all the time.

"Amen," John say one day. "I have a story to share, a
new one as fresh as a spring blossom."

"My ears, friend, are big," say Amen.

And that's when John, he smile and what Amen
seen was happy gums.

"I have seen the end and the beginning, the omega
and the alpha," John say. "I have written it on a scroll.
There is something you should hear."

Amen swallow what he had in his mouth.

Then John go on, "He in the long robe, he with hair
and a face as white as snow showed me. His voice was

like the sound of rushing water. The end is terrible and good. The fibber will have his due."

"I don't like the fibber," say Amen. "He is the enemy of hope."

John, he nod for he know that, too. Then he say, "It will be a great and awful reckoning."

"When?" ask Amen.

But John, he just show him his gums again. "Amen, you have been faithful."

"I have tried to be led well."

"It is better to be led than pushed," say John. "You will be led some more, good donkey."

And what happen next is John laugh so hard, he cry, and what he done also was wheeze, he try to catch his breath so much.

Amen, he din't know nothing about that. He just take another bite and swish his tail for to swish away a fly.

Finally, John scratch Amen behind the ears and smooth his coat real nice and say, "Amen. Let it be done. Do you know why, of all the other animals, you were given the ability to speak to man?"

Amen say no.

"I'll tell you," say John. "As a donkey, you are well-suited to carry heavy loads. The load you carry now is a story: words strung together since the beginning, invisible cargo on the back of a humble beast. I have seen the end of this story. I have only seen glimpses of the next."

"I am a storyteller?" ask Amen.

"Yes, and a guardian, too."

Amen tell me he shake his head hard at that.

"How am I well suited to be a guardian?"

"You are stubborn. You won't forget. You won't give in to time. You haven't yet."

Amen think about what John say for a minute,

and then he ask, "But to whom? I have learned a lot
about man. He can be a cruel master. There were times
when I kept my words to myself. Some men only hear
their own stories. And worse, some men only hear lies.
I know a story that can free them from their torments.
Who can hear it, though, with the fibber taking them
for long walks in the desert?"

John rub Amen's withers, and it feel good. "Yes,
yes," he start gently. "The fibber is persistent. But what
is his persistence next to the truth you carry?"

"I know the strength of his tug."

"You have also felt his release, unwilling though it
was."

"Thank God."

"Yes, and praise."

Amen *he-haw* 'cause whatever he think to say, it
din't work.

"My brothers and I aren't the only ones charged
with relaying the good news."

"I am a donkey. I talk. You say it is to tell a story—
one I've lived, one I carry."

"Yes," say John. "You have been entrusted."

"Please tell me then: Who will listen?"

"Those who can."

"Those who can?"

"Those who wouldn't think it that strange or that
impossible to hear a donkey speak."

"I don't understand."

John take a minute before he speak again. "Not
everybody is so sure about the world around them.
For those far in the desert, weak and disheartened by
the fibber's tugs, don't fret. There are other messengers,
other ways. But you, dear friend, are specially equipped.
You are message and messenger both."

"I know what happened to you in Rome," say
Amen 'cause what it was was he pretend he was with

the animals there so he can see what happen to John. "And I know what happened to your friends."

"Killed," John say. "Yes."

"A fate I don't think I can ever know. But the story is still the same."

"A story that must be told."

"The messengers, some were killed brutally."

"And this is why you must press into the coming darkness. The message you carry is hated. It is contrary to the lies that have gripped creation. But you are a donkey that speaks, an animal, just so. You are contrary yourself. The message is safe where it is assumed it doesn't exist."

Amen think for a little bit then he say, "I know the story, and I am happy to tell it. It is the very least I can do. But it is not like I can stand amongst the crowd and speak out. I cannot write on scrolls." He look down at his hooves.

John sigh and that sigh turn into a calm smile. He smooth Amen's withers again. "Those who can, those still left alone by the worst of doubt—they will find you."

"They will find me?"

"They will look upon you, and even if they don't say it, the sense of recognition will wax across their faces."

Wax means grow, not like what a candle is, and I know this 'cause I ask.

Amen, he just say, "They will never have seen me before."

"Not so," say John. "We have all seen your likes. You echo our home in common." And after that, John, he walk away 'cause he finish telling Amen what he want to say to him.

They leaned opposite each other against the barn doorjambs. The blocky shade from the barn slinked imperceptibly over the ground. "So then he came to Kentucky?" asked Spring-baby.

"That was a long time ago when he talk to John," replied Chirp Vanhoosen. He uncrossed his long legs then crossed them again the other way.

Spring-baby pushed her bangs away from her eyes—tried to push them behind her ears—but they swung back into their original place anyway. "He got on a boat or something, found good owners, and waited for the right people to find him?"

"He got on a boat when John tell him it was time to go."

"Then he came here."

"He leave John way before he come to Kentucky. Remember he just poof, and there, I seen him."

Spring-baby thought about what she had said. "I didn't mean he came right here. I mean Amen just told the story and helped people out when he did."

"He tell the story alright."

"I want to see him."

"He's not here now."

"How do I find him?"

"I dunno."

"Why won't he poof for me? I don't doubt anymore. I want to see Amen. I want him to tell me the story."

"I dunno how," said Chirp Vanhoosen at a loss.

Spring-baby tried once more with the bangs. "I'm too far in the desert," she decided.

Chirp Vanhoosen scratched his head, rubbed his nose, didn't make a sound.

"That's why he won't come," she continued. "I threw a rock and blew my chance."

Her feebleminded companion remained reticent, unable, perhaps, to find the words to steer her away from a sense of total depravity.

"I have to go work," he said finally. He entered the barn, sad in the knowledge that she probably wouldn't follow.

XXVI

There was nothing left for Spring-baby to do but think. She had been abandoned, each person falling away either by fate or fatigue, and what she was left with was merely herself: a girl laden with questions she could not answer, ones she could not even articulate. Who would have her? What could they say? The chasm walls around her vaulted into the sky and blocked out the sun. Nobody could rescue her. Not really, at least. She had discovered what truth there is in living, ultimately—that the big things make hermits of us all. Birth and love. Growing old. Death. We face these things singularly, and in the end, we are dwarfed by them, cornered, shut off with nowhere to go but into the fray. Spring-baby was just in this place. So she decided to walk.

She walked out of the pasture and out of the yard. A road ran parallel to her grandparents' property. She walked on the gravelly shoulder between the pavement and the ditch. Few cars and trucks passed by. The day was hot, the air, summer sweet.

She kicked stones as she walked. When the road she was following intersected with the train tracks, she changed her course. In one direction, the tracks vanished around a curve while in the other direction they drew up to a point on the horizon. It was toward that point she walked, taking giant steps from one railway tie to another.

Overhead, a crow cawed its presence before alighting on the uppermost branch of a pine tree then announcing itself again. On one side of the tracks, something scurried away beneath the buzzing, chaotic weeds. Spring-baby continued to travel in this manner—one big step after another—until she got tired, at which point she tried her skill at balancing on a rail as if it were a long metal tightrope. She held her arms out to the sides and carefully laid each foot heel to toe. She was good at the game, for she only lost her balance once, landing without incident in the wide, rough bed of fist-sized rocks that supported the rail line. Soon, though, this bit of caprice wearied her, so she leaped off the rail and plodded clumsily along over rocks that were too big and ties that were too far apart. Two thin lines of trees enclosed the railroad tracks, allowing Spring-baby glances at houses along the way, but as she walked on, the lines became denser, the hum of the weeds louder until it was clear that the railroad tracks had led her into a thick stretch of woods.

Spring-baby continued to walk regardless. Only when she spied a creek winding shyly through the trees on one side of the tracks did she leave the soothing monotony of following a path spiked resolutely to the earth.

The brook sparkled where the sunrays struck and was placid where they did not. Spring-baby descended from the tracks, made her way over loose dirt and rocks and through a small tangle of saplings and blackberry bushes to a bend in the brook where the water slowed down and pooled before gushing into a narrow length that flowed tight against a bulging bank.

Spring-baby tossed the first stone she found into the middle of the pool and watched the rings of water expand until they quietly sloshed against the shore. Then she tossed in another stone, this one heavy enough for her to need both hands, but it fell far short of the center of the pool and instead made a splash that got her feet a little wet. But when she reached down again, she caught small movement out of the corner of her eye, causing her to stop mid-motion, kneel, and crane her neck to find out what it was.

A frog no bigger than a quarter hopped from one flat rock to the next in the intent way frogs do. And not far from that frog, another frog rested on top of a rock shaped like an ostrich egg. As Spring-baby scanned the area around her, she discovered other frogs either sitting or hopping along in various directions.

She peered out across the water. The pool beckoned her with its unmolested stillness. She hesitated for only a second then carefully cupped a frog from a rock and stood with it bouncing in her hands. At the water's edge, she tossed the frog into the pool then watched it begin to paddle to the opposite shore, making almost imperceptible ripples as it went.

First, she lobbed a pebble, watching it plunk beneath the water a few feet from the frog. But the second missile was bigger, fell closer, and created enough of a splash for the frog to notice and paddle away from the disturbance. The tiny frog was about a yard from solid ground when the third rock struck and swelled the water so much that the frog momentarily flipped over on its back before righting itself and continuing its frantic push toward shore. Spring-baby picked up a large, flat rock, its underside damp and muddy, and closed the distance between herself and the frog as much as she could without completely submerging her sneakers. She remembered how Chirp Vanhoosen hoisted the larger rocks from the wheelbarrow to the weeds. She widened her stance just as he had done, and she bent her knees slightly, too. Then, with a soft grunt, she heaved

the rock toward the swimming frog. The rock did not twist
in the air but remained even and true, and when it hit the
frog, it did so with a slap then disappeared beneath the surface.
Before the water stilled, the little frog floated to the top, belly
up and dead.

She readily found another frog and tossed it into the pool.
This, she hit in a single blow with another large, flat rock.
Spring-baby was making a game of it. A half dozen frogs later,
she remained insatiable, her appetite for dispatching frogs in
this way robust.

She was about to throw another frog into the pool when
from the growth behind her came the crunchy, rustling sound
of feet scampering over twigs and loose leaves. She turned
and laid her eyes on a groundhog, plump and as white as
cotton, emerging from beneath a cacophony of blackberry
bushes.

Upon seeing her, the groundhog stopped and propped itself
up on two hind legs, letting its forepaws dangle uselessly in
front. It stared, and its piercing red albino eyes issued forth an
intelligence Spring-baby had never seen in an animal.

"I've been watching you the whole time," said the groundhog sternly by way of introduction.

Spring-baby dropped the frog she was cupping, paying it
no heed as it hurriedly hopped away over the rocky shore.

"Why are you being so cruel?" it continued. After a
moment, it dropped to all fours, took a few casual steps
forward, then propped itself up again. It was a convincing
entreaty.

Spring-baby stepped back, accidentally placing a foot into
the water. "You're a groundhog," she said not a little apprehen-
sively.

"And you're a cruel little girl. I would have stepped out
of the brush earlier had I been certain that you wouldn't have
dealt me the same treatment. But watching you—I eventually
figured I was a bit too big for you to handle."

"You talk."

"Yes, and I'm telling you that lobbing rocks on little frogs is mean, and you shouldn't ever do it." A front paw came up and seemed to brush away an annoyance from near its mouth.

Spring-baby retrieved her foot from the water, didn't bother to shake it off. "I've never heard a groundhog talk or any other animal even."

"Well, you're hearing one now."

"I've always wanted to," she stammered, "hear an animal talk."

"You shouldn't ever do that to frogs," repeated the groundhog, then for good measure, he added, "Or any other animal even."

"I know. I'm sorry."

"Why do you think that's fun?"

"I don't know."

"You don't know?"

"I was just doing it, I guess. I don't know why."

The groundhog grunted its disapproval. "You're awfully fond of throwing rocks, aren't you?"

"I know it's wrong," said Spring-baby shamefully.

"Big rocks at frogs, littler rocks at donkeys."

"Amen?"

"You don't think I know? A squirrel's gossip travels fast."

"Squirrels talk, too?"

"Little girl," began the groundhog with summoned patience, "you need to pay more attention. Why is it that your kind believes they are the only ones with anything important to say?"

"I didn't know."

The groundhog squinted keenly. "You don't seem to know much, do you?"

"I'm only twelve."

"Some knowledge has little to do with years." Then as if aroused by the warm breeze that gently swayed the tips of some nearby wild barley, it erected its back some more, sniffed the air, and looked about intently.

"Do you know Amen?" Spring-baby asked, hoping to recapture the groundhog's attention.

It looked left then right, nose searching the air, before relaxing and resuming its study of the little girl. "I've nibbled clover in his pasture on more than one occasion. He's a wise old donkey with many stories to tell."

"I know some," said Spring-baby.

"I thought you never heard an animal speak before."

"I haven't. Chirp Vanhoosen is the one that takes care of Amen. He's the one that tells me. He's heard Amen speak, but not me."

"Chirp Vanhoosen, eh?"

"He's slow, but I like talking to him anyways."

"He tells you the stories?"

"Yes. I haven't seen Amen since…" She stopped abruptly and averted her eyes because she imagined the groundhog already knew when.

"I always figured Chirp Vanhoosen was a good one to listen. He doesn't let himself get in the way of the truth, if you know what I mean."

Spring-baby looked up like she might know, but soon her countenance changed, and the groundhog probably surmised that she didn't.

The groundhog moved close enough for Spring-baby to reach out and stroke its white fur had she been so inclined. Its whiskers jerked excitedly. It reassumed its stance on its back haunches and looked straight up at her and spoke.

"When you were a baby, your daddy would put you on the floor to play. You'd crawl about, explore, discover the good and the bad. Sometimes you'd bump your head and cry. Other times you'd laugh with glee when your daddy would get down with you and tickle your chin, hum a pretty tune, tell you again how much he loved you. When your daddy thought it was time, he'd reach down for you, and when you'd see him do it, you'd smile and reach up for him because you knew he'd keep you safe and secure as he'd wrap you in his arms.

"Chirp Vanhoosen is a good one to listen because he knows he has nothing to fear. You were like that once. But one day, you forgot that someone was looking down on you, and you imagined you were alone. For many like you, this comes with getting old, so as hairs gray and bodies grow heavier, the end becomes a terrifying unknown. But for those like Chirp Vanhoosen, a good one to listen, the end is simply a return. There's comfort in that knowledge. We are not alone."

The groundhog waited, its nose twitching patiently, but when Spring-baby did not speak, it fell upon a single dandelion, munching pleasantly as if Spring-baby were not even standing there.

Spring-baby waited politely for the groundhog to swallow. "Do you have a name?"

This time, upon hearing Spring-baby's voice, the groundhog picked up its head in utter shock. The look was gone from its eyes. No more was there a look of rare sagacity in its face. Instead a wildness seemed to repossess the rodent, and before Spring-baby could say anything else, the groundhog dashed into the brush with a squeal.

She ran up to the point of entry, but it was no use, for the animal was nowhere to be seen. She looked around for only a second or two but decided she was in no mood to dawdle. She raced back up the small hill to the tracks and sprinted over the ties and rocks as best she could until she got to the road that ran in front of her grandparents' home. Spring-baby ran until she was out of breath, relieved by what the groundhog had shared, hoping she had not imagined the whole encounter.

XXVII

Between each gulp and release of air Spring-baby relayed what had happened, her small frame expanding and contracting all the while.

"We are all just babies crawling on the floor!" she said.

Chirp Vanhoosen took a sideways look at the little girl. "No groundhog tell you that," he said.

"But it did."

"Only Amen can talk to people. Remember what John say?"

"You think I'm lying."

"No. But Amen, he don't lie, and he tell me that he's the only one that can talk like us."

"We are not alone, and when it's time, God picks us up," insisted Spring-baby.

Chirp Vanhoosen smiled. "I know what that is."

"Way away."

But Chirp Vanhoosen's smile quickly spoiled, and his face contorted in an attempt to understand Spring-baby's claim about the albino groundhog. Surely she was upset with Amen for not poofing for her, but any notion of another pontificating animal did not add up to what he had come to accept about the donkey's uniqueness. He felt bad for the girl. He wished Amen would poof for her. But it simply wasn't a matter on which he could weigh in. He didn't know where Amen was, and he certainly didn't know what to say in response to what was probably a fanciful, albeit wishful delusion.

Chirp Vanhoosen's sudden change in countenance did not escape Spring-baby's notice. "What was it, then?"

"I dunno what was it."

Spring-baby swallowed the saliva that had collected in her mouth. "I was angry or bored or I just wanted to," she began, "but I threw rocks at some frogs I had tossed into the water."

"Rocks?"

"I know it was bad."

"You throw rocks at Amen."

"Yes."

"You hit him, and I yell at you, but you, you run away."

"I came back."

"But he go away then." He biffed a splinter he had absently dug out of a plank into the air.

"Poofed."

Chirp Vanhoosen nodded slowly, unsurely. "You tell me how we're all babies crawling."

"It's what the groundhog said."

"I'm not very smart, but I know what I hear," said Chirp Vanhoosen quite obviously at a loss. "I hear that about babies before, and that's us, really."

Spring-baby smiled.

"But that Francis, he din't throw rocks. He did a lot, lot more bad."

Amen, he try to tell lots of people the story, but he find out they was too far gone, so somebody else had to try to tell them. Every now and then, he'd tell a little boy or a little girl, but they was so little that they din't know what they was hearing.

Amen, he din't stop. Them Romans what I tell you about, they was boss over a lot of land, and the people that live there din't like that at all. But Amen, what he did was travel around in that land from stall to stall, pasture to pasture to pasture, for there was new roads built, and more and more people come from far off. They trade what they grow or make and sometimes they need a donkey for to carry it all. Amen was smart how he got around and tell the story. He got lucky every now and then, but mostly what he did was keep moving, sometimes getting selled, sometimes he just run off.

Then Amen get a surprise. A stranger walk right up to Amen on the street when Amen was tie up and waiting for his owner. The stranger say to Amen, "I was a soldier, then a prisoner, and now I'm a servant of God."

The stranger had on a long brown robe and sandals, and his hair on the top of his head was gone. He talk right at Amen like he know Amen can understand him. "It is possible. As everything is with Him."

"I've seen as much," say Amen.

"So I understand."

When the owner come back, the stranger, he convince him for to borrow Amen for a bit, and 'cause the owner was a good owner, and he din't need Amen right then, he say okay, just bring him back. He was okay with friars. (That's somebody that's all they do is stuff for God.)

The friar tell Amen his name was Francis, and he been looking for him, for that morning he wake up thinking he had to tell something to a special donkey, and that something he figger out was his own story about how he was a soldier, and how he got caught, and what he learn.

"I killed men," say Francis. "I witnessed the evil man is capable of."

"I've been beaten and cast into the dark, cold, and wet. I know what you say. I've lived it, too."

"Amen," go on Francis real sad, "I feasted on the blood of my enemies. I reveled in their misery. Why? I don't know. I was a happy youth. I had noble dreams, I thought. Perhaps it was the ambition that did it. I became a soldier on my own when others were forced because I thought myself the better man for volunteering. But I was a fool. When I picked up the sword, I laid down all humility. Was it pride that led to my own walk in wickedness?" (That was when Francis laugh, Amen say.) "I suppose. It's common enough. But why I learned to enjoy it, I'll never know."

"The ways of the evil one are tricky. It is best not to battle the fibber alone."

"You are right. I know. The evil one is a brilliant tactician. Divide and conquer—my questions from God's answers. Most of the battle is in the mind."

"Solitude in that way can lead to only one end."

"Yes, but solitude in another way can yield desirable results."

"True."

"I was held in captivity for a year, and it was during that time I discovered wickedness for what it was: not me but a vestment sneakily draped around me."

"It was grace that freed you."

Francis smile real wide, and Amen think he was

going to laugh again, but he din't and even his expression on his face change to not smiling at all. "I hear praises everywhere," he go on. "God's creatures flock to me, and I can understand every one."

"You understand *me*."

"And cardinals and robins and jays that perch on my shoulders. And deer and fox that creep out of the forest. And fish that harmonize their voices with the chatter of streams. And rabbits that emerge from their warrens, bubbling over with good things to say."

"It is a din, for sure, but a joyous one."

"I could have lived my life in dismal silence, Amen. I could have walked by the chorus and never heard the song. I should have confessed to you earlier that this is not the first time I laid eyes upon you. I saw you hitched to a cart in which were piled the bodies of the slain. We both were on one side of a great contest. You looked up at me forlornly as if you were simply trying to endure."

"I was. I thought you looked familiar. Yes, I remember how you seemed to search me as if I could explain the horrors we were witnessing."

"Could you?"

"I could offer hope. I've glimpsed the end of death and destruction, and it is good."

"There was something about you out of all the other beasts that arrested my attention. It's funny. I was damaged, yet I could still recognize salvation or at least its messenger."

"I have a strong back, and the rumor about my being stubborn is true."

They had walk a long, long ways, and by then they was way into the forest that was outside the village. Amen notice birds was flying nearby like they was following, and some deers and a few rabbits was tagging along and not even trying to hide.

That was when Amen, he say, "I talk best when I'm walking. Oh, the walks I've taken."

"Yes?"

Then Amen tell Francis about it all, from Adam on up. Prob'ly he leave out some stuff, for the story, it's a long one, but Amen say Francis din't seem to mind just sitting against a tree and listening. Francis ask some questions, and Amen answer them. There was animals and birds all around like a crowd, but they was just listening, too, and that was fine with Amen.

When Amen got done telling his story, Francis say, "In the garden, there was kinship with the animals until Eve disobeyed. Then there was slaughter so that the two could use animal skins to cover up their nakedness. With Noah, the animals, and not the other men, were brought into the safety of the ark. This was God's decree, for surely had man decided who should be on board, there would not have been space made for even a mouse. And then there came Jesus, dear Jesus. Delivered to His birth on a donkey, delivered to His death on the same."

"You listen well."

"I see brutality against man and creature alike, and I wonder how reconciliation is possible. But I admit, I am trapped by the flesh so must rely on faith that better days are ahead." He look all around at the animals that had got together. "I am buoyed."

"Sometimes faith is all we got."

Francis, he reach over and stroke a cottontail behind the ears, but it was like he was thinking real hard. "Perhaps faith is a condition best understood by children, for when does a person see clearest but as an infant?"

"Agreed," say Amen, and he din't have to think no more about it.

"To secure that simplicity of heart," go on Francis,

"exist in it, breath it in, be at peace, makes the quest for it small by comparison."

Amen, he shake his shaggy mane. "It is a difficult journey to get back to where we started, Francis," say Amen. "But permit me to say this: when I was deep in the desert with the fibber, tired and beaten, not knowing yet where I was being led, I rested in a fact that can never change."

"What fact is this?"

"What was happening to me happened before. There was a model for my trial."

"I see."

"The fibber is fond of whisking people away and bribing them with lies."

"He is a wedge."

"Yes, jealous and cruel."

"I admire your wisdom, Amen," say Francis. "Your calmness of spirit." Then he din't say nothing else after that, but finally he say, "I was at the market not a week ago, and I was pondering my new ability to hear and to understand the praises sung by all creation when I happened upon a man thrashing a mutt tied to a stake. The dog had blood on its hide. It yelped ferociously. I called to the man to stop but was met with such a violent flurry of curses as to fear for my own well-being. I walked away, ignoring the dog's pleading eyes, and I covered my ears as the man resumed the beating."

"It is horrible what men sometimes do."

Francis nod. "But don't you see? I, too, was part of that evil. I did nothing. I was afraid, so I walked on. How can I reach for innocence, possess the faith of a child, speak to others about it, when I am the architect of my own ruin?"

Then he laugh, what Amen say, and it was a nervous laugh.

"I've been blessed, yet I do not know what to do

with this gift in a world so dominated by everything bad. The vestment of sin is burdensome. I wonder if it is too much."

Amen, he tell me that this was prob'ly why Francis was tell to come find him, for Francis, he was having a hard time making sense of what he seen in his life and what he could do now, talk and listen to the animals.

"Your concern is with your ability to stand for what is right in the face of so much sin, inside and out."

"I am unworthy of this gift. I learned what wickedness is during my time in captivity, and for that knowledge, I am grateful. I took up the cloth as a result, thinking I would lead a life of quiet contemplation. But I stand corrected. With this gift, I fear I am called upon not simply to be a studious servant but also to be a guide, an example for how we're meant to be as one kind out of a multitude of kinds all equally given the breath of God."

"We all have our tasks."

"I do not begrudge mine."

And what that means is he's not mad about it.

"But I do confess to you my fear."

"You are forgiven."

"I am forgiven."

"But do you know what that means?"

(Amen, he tell me Francis go to say something, but in the end, he din't.)

"It is the biggest, most important part of the story I must tell," say Amen.

"I *thought* I knew what it meant," say Francis. "Please share your thoughts with one so new on the path to God."

Amen look at the friar sitting there with all them animals around him: bunnies that was curl up next to him, deers eating from tufts of grass by the tree, squirrels and even chipmunks, some of them racing up and down the trunk, some of them not. Amen think about the gift Francis got, and he wonder for why he got it, then he wonder really why Francis was scared and all.

"You've seen much of the evil the world is capable of," say Amen.

"A wide variety, I have," reply Francis.

"And now that your ears are attuned to the array of voices in creation, you doubt your worthiness to receive such a gift and the commission it entails."

(Me, I had to stop Amen there and ask questions, and what he say was Francis, his gift come with a job, and that was to tell everybody how the world could be, and when Amen say that to me, I understand.)

Francis, he had no problem understanding it 'cause he say, "I am a simple man who has seen and done too much. My sins are forgiven. I know this—"

But Amen, he interrupt and say, "And that means what, Francis?"

"That I have been made clean."

"That sin, past and present, is powerless over you. You are reconciled, meaning that the journey to God is but one single step forward. It is a difficult step, but a single one nonetheless. Innocence, a heart in the right place, all those things you want and that will both free and equip you, can be had with a single word. Your true heart isn't as far away as you think."

"Yes?"

Amen, he shake his head yes, his muzzle go all the way up and all the way down, then he just go on, he tell me, watching a ton of bricks come off of that friar.

"You said a groundhog didn't talk to me," said Spring-baby. "You told me how only Amen can speak to people. All kinds of animals spoke to Francis."

"Francis, he understand all kinds of animals, but they din't speak right to *him*."

Spring-baby issued a quick, annoyed grunt. "You're teasing me."

"I ain't."

"So the groundhog said the same thing to me as Amen did to that Francis."

"It's what I tell you."

"But you don't think I heard anything."

"I din't tell you that."

"Then who told me then?"

He considered the question with an uneasy sway of his head. "Prob'ly God," he offered finally.

"An albino groundhog?"

"God was a drop of water. He was a voice. He even become a man that got kilt."

"But why?"

"When you leave, you leave mad for you think you blow your chances for to talk to Amen. You throw rocks. Even you seen death, and that makes it hard to believe."

"So?"

"Francis seen a lot and prob'ly lots of it death, too. But Amen, he teach Francis that even he seen so much, he can be a child again. Not a real one but where it counts."

"Okay," she said, trying to follow.

"So I think what Francis learn, you should learn, too."

"I need to be like a child again. I already know."

"Yes, but do you know like what you need to? All what makes you sad and me, too, prob'ly" said Chirp Vanhoosen, not really looking at Spring-baby so much as he was looking through her. "It's been done with. No more. At all. If we want, we can be children for always."

Like Francis, thought Spring-baby, *who was spoken to way before Kentucky but on soil all the same.*

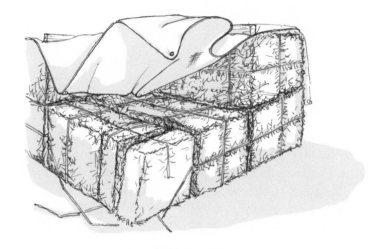

XXVIII

Stacked against the wall toward the back of the barn were small bales of straw covered with a dirty blue tarpaulin. Random lengths and cuts of two-by-fours weighed down the tarpaulin, and an assortment of other boards, some with nails still sticking through them, leaned against a corner of the mound in a loose bundle. After he finished his thought with Spring-baby, Chirp Vanhoosen got to work by removing the boards, pulling away the tarpaulin, and hurling some bales toward the open entrance of a vacant stall, thinking, perhaps, that Spring-baby would respond in her own good time. When enough bales were thrown from the stack, he stood by the new pile, and with a jackknife he extracted from a leather case attached to his belt, cut the twine binding each bale and scattered the straw around the inside of the stall.

"Isn't that where Amen stays?" asked Spring-baby from where she sat on an overturned bucket.

"This stall, it's for a horse. The horse'll be here soon."

Spring-baby stood up and drifted toward the open stall door. She watched as Chirp Vanhoosen cut the twine from another bale and spread the straw generously. "I don't want to ever get old," she said.

"I'm twenty-five and a half," said Chirp Vanhoosen. "For my birthday, I want a new jackknife 'cause this one I got a real long time ago."

"We'll all go way away sometime."

"It's what happens," replied Chirp Vanhoosen, looking up only briefly.

"I know," said Spring-baby. "Today, an albino groundhog—God, I guess—told me how to be a good one to listen. There is nothing to be afraid of, he said. I am not alone."

"And me, too. I'm not either."

"Yes. And neither was Francis. Or anybody else."

"Francis, he understand animals."

Spring-baby caught Chirp Vanhoosen's eyes. "Was he buried? Like my dad and your mom?"

"In the ground?"

"We all go way away. Even if we say yes like Francis did and become children for always, we all get picked up from the floor eventually."

"It's what I say," said Chirp Vanhoosen, flinging a handful of straw.

"You don't get it," said Spring-baby. "For my last birthday, I got a dress. I wanted a toy, but I got a dress I was only supposed to wear on Sundays. It was white and had small flowers on it. It was one size too big."

"You'll get more bigger."

Spring-baby sighed, approaching exasperation. "I'll get bigger. Yes."

"You can wear the dress." By this time, Chirp Vanhoosen had stopped what he was doing and stood there in the middle of the stall, trying to figure out what he and Spring-baby were discussing.

"You want me to go to bed and wake up yesterday morning."

"I don't get it."

"That's because it's easy for you."

"What is?"

"Being . . . being happy about it all."

"Going where we're going?"

Spring-baby clutched the bottom of her shirt and pulled it downward, tightening it over her budding breasts. "I had hopes."

"To be happy."

"For Judd Wade."

"Who's he?"

"He's in my grade. He moved up from Georgia, and he lives with his grandparents, and they live next door to us."

"A boy?"

She grinned a little. "Yes. We have a shed behind our house. Inside there's the lawnmower and some garden tools, and in the winter, that's where my bike goes."

"Like the barn's for."

"I suppose," she said, then looked around some as if she had never before been on the inside of the barn. "We called it our hideout. A week before my dad died, we shut ourselves in the shed. The only light came from the cracks between where the roof met the wall. I couldn't even see the color of his hair. I knew, though, that he was chewing Big Red."

"That's gum."

"I was shaking, and so was he. I had hopes. He talked different from anybody else at school. But in the end, he just pushed open the door and ran away, and when I found him later, he was trying to throw a flat basketball into a hoop with no net. My dad had put up the hoop before he went away. The basketball had been left outside over the winter."

"You like Judd Wade."

She nodded pensively, then she said, "I never kissed anyone on the lips until I kissed my dad at the funeral home."

Chirp Vanhoosen had never kissed anybody on the lips at all, but he knew what she meant. "There's only one first time," he said. "It's all we can ever get."

"I have cold lips to remember. They're what I still feel when you tell me how easy it is to be a child. Maybe it is easy." Her head started to shake as if of its own volition. "But not for me. Everywhere I look, I see grownups. And I know that's where I'm heading. Maybe I'll smoke in the bathroom, or maybe when I learn to drive, I'll go find my own butterflies."

"That's sad."

"That's easiest."

"For why?"

"It's the only thing I can be sure of."

Chirp Vanhoosen sucked in a lungful of air, wanted to challenge Spring-baby but didn't know how.

"Later today, the sun will go down," Spring-baby continued. "And tomorrow will be another step in the wrong direction. This is what happens. I'm already like my grandparents. I'm already like my mother and my uncle."

"Them, they need to hear the story from somewhere else and not a donkey."

"Fine. But you can't hope against the hours. What's done is done. Judd Wade will never be my first. I can't make myself believe he was."

Chirp Vanhoosen sighed deeply then moved to grab another small bale of straw but ultimately decided against it. He chose, instead, to look at the work he had done and wait.

"There's no reason to come down here anymore," said Spring-baby finally. "When it's my turn, I'll be buried in the ground, too."

"Amen, he got to here after Francis," said Chirp Vanhoosen quickly. "Don'tcha wanna know how?"

She stopped, turned. "It's been a nice story," she said, trying to smile. "Still the best I've ever heard."

XXIX

The people, there was more and more of them, and what Amen tell me, all those people keep on wondering what else is out there that they could get for themselves, even they had all they need already. The people talk, and they write down what they say, too, and some grow real serious about it all. They put together armies that fight each other till the ground got soak with blood. Sometimes Amen, he got drag into the fighting for to pull carts and carry the dead, but sometimes he din't. He just hear all what was going on around him—talking, fighting, people that cry and even whisper, "What else is there? What else can I get?" When the towns become cities, people, they still ask it. Amen, he only talk to a few people at

that time, but what the people ask was more loud than
Amen, so soon, he become a donkey that all he does is
he-haw and do what he's tell.

Amen carry what fat men own. He pull plows with
other donkeys up and down great big fields. He sleep
in stalls when outside it was raining, and kids got wet
'cause they din't have no roof like he did.

One time, he say, "Come inside, children, where
it's warm and dry." Only them kids, they was so tired
out and dirty and look like they seen a lot even they
was little, Amen say, they couldn't understand, and that
make Amen sad.

That was still in Italy where it happened about the
children. But Amen, he go all over, across mountains
and over seas for to see who could believe that a donkey
can talk.

He find a gypsy boy that all he did was whistle
for to say something. Amen, he just run away from a
farmer that was real poor even the floor in his house
was dirt and he seem to wanna take all his deep, dark
anger out on Amen's back. So Amen run into the
woods for to hide, and he keep walking, and then he
seen smoke, and before he could go away from that, he
hear a whistle, and what Amen say, it was good 'cause
he know what it mean.

The boy, he stand down by a creek that Amen just
got a drink from, and the boy, he din't look mean or
nothing, just nice like he wasn't no stranger.

He whistle again, and Amen, he tell me it sound
like a bird in the morning, and when I ask what that
means, Amen say, hope; it sound like hope.

Amen feel fine about walking up to the boy, so
that's what he did, and when he got close, the boy, he
reach out and pet Amen and even take a handful of
grass that he pick and feed him, too.

Then he whistle soft. It was a whistle that float

around Amen's muzzle, twist up around his ears, and
settle on the rest of his body like snow.

Amen say to the boy, "Why won't you talk to me?"

But the boy just whistle again.

"Is it because you can't?"

But the boy just smile.

Amen, he want to go on asking questions, but all
the sudden a great big man with a red face and eyes
like the stones he seen at the bottom of the creek come
crashing down by where they was, and he was yelling at
the boy to get more wood for the fire.

"We're down to coals!" he scream, and then he grab
the boy by the arm real hard and shake him till Amen
did hear another sound from the boy, and it was a
whimper 'cause he was scared. The man pay Amen no
mind, he was so angry. When he drag the boy away,
Amen hear all what the man was going to do to the
boy, and it was ugly, ugly! Amen just tell me that, and I
din't ask what the man really say.

Amen, he go away from the smoke, but it din't take
him long for to find the answer to what he ask the
boy. He ask the boy can you talk. Amen figger the boy,
he could, but if all he hear was words that was bad
and full of hate, then that's all he thought words ever
was. Anyhow, Amen understand what the boy mean
when he whistle. It's what I say about the birds in the
morning sounding like hope. Sometimes it seem it's the
littlest around that give us that, is what Amen say.

On and on there was fires that burn down the
towns, and people, they got sick, and lots got put in
the ground or take away and throw on burn piles like
what I do to the leaves that fall and I rake up. Amen
pull all that can be pull and carry all that can be
carry. He was with armies that walk for miles for
to just destroy all they seen except what they want.
He was with other donkeys and horses and men—all

of them going between towns and cities and even countries, trading, fighting, running away, and fighting some more. Amen, he tell me many people, they believe the lies that the fibber tell. It was hard for Amen for to find someone to listen, but every now and then, he did.

There was a town in Spain, and what lots of the people there did was fish. A man trade Amen for five jugs of wine and a girl that had black teeth, but she can work and don't cry. The man that got Amen, he live in a shack that you can see the ocean from. Every day, he put baskets of fish on Amen's back and selled the fish in town. When it got dark out, the man, he tie Amen up to a little tree, give Amen food and water, and drink wine and talk when nobody's there.

Sometimes, the man, he got a bottle when he was in town, and he drink it all the way to the shack. Those times, he forget to give Amen his food and water and also he din't tie him up. There was other shacks out there that you can see the ocean from. In one was a boy name Juan Jo. What Juan Jo did was give fish to what's call the *los gatos del mar*.

That's something I din't know. Amen say it's "the cats of the sea."

Every time when it almost was dark out, Juan Jo, he sneak out of his shack and go down by the ocean, and there they was, all these cats that come out from where they sleep and eat what he bring them. Amen could hear all the meows, and he say they was happy ones for prob'ly their stomachs was growling, and they wait all day for them to not growl.

Amen always watch when Juan Jo take down the fish to the *los gatos del mar*. There was a time when the man that sell the fish, he got two bottles in town and drink them all the way home, and that was when Amen walk down to see the boy.

"Why do you give food to these creatures?" ask
Amen. "They can give you nothing in return."

Juan Jo, he look up from the basket only a little
surprise, but after he put another fish down in front of
the cats, he say, "My father was in the war. When he
died, my mother went crazy and could not take care of
me. I live with my uncle. He is a fisherman. Without
him, I would have to beg on the streets."

"Your uncle is good to you?"

"I have nothing to give to him in return."

And what Amen tell me, a cat rub against his leg,
and Juan Jo, he reach down and pet him with tears in
his eyes.

Amen meet Juan Jo almost every night after that,
for nobody wanted to do business with a drunk, and
that make the man that put baskets of fish on Amen's
back want more wine. So, Amen, he din't get tie up at
all after a while. Even he help Juan Jo to take down
the fish. Amen seen all the colors of cats—calico, and
ones with white tips on their tails like waves that Amen
see crest in the sea.

The people, they build boats that was great big and
had sails that look like clouds in the sky. But Amen
say they was really storm clouds, for they carry thunder
wherever they go.

People keep on asking, "What else is there? What
else can I get?" They look at each other for to get
the answer, and when they got tired of that, they look
across the ocean and dream it might be there.

What it began like was Amen, he just hear stories
about strange lands and strange people, but before he
know it, he got sweep up in it all—he got traded, and
buyed, and taken—till the next thing that happen, he's
on one of them boats with clouds, and he's tie down
below where the people pray against the water that hit
against the sides.

Amen, he pull plows on land he never seen before, but he tell me that it wasn't strange at all. Even he seen the people that was call strange, but he din't think so about them. And what else, Amen, he say that lots of them what was call savages can hear him and listen to the story.

"Tell us your secrets," they say. "You have walked a long ways with madmen."

"I have walked a long ways," say Amen. "This is true. But what you call madness, I call the despair of broken men. I am a storyteller. I go where the story needs to be told."

But them what was called savages din't stick around for to listen to Amen. The madmen come more and more, and them savages din't have time to listen to a donkey, for all they had to do just to get along.

Amen tell me about hard times. He tell me about bloodshed and sickness, about all the bad things people can do to other people.

The people there got to be more of them. They make more towns and cities and keep going out towards where the sun goes down. And Amen, either he run away or get selled, he go with them, too.

Like what I say about how Amen was tie inside the boat, for he can't go nowhere, so was people brung from far away like that same way. And they was make to do work even they don't want to. Small Henry was make to clean stables, chop wood, fetch water, and lots more than that. Amen seen Small Henry for the first time when Small Henry run into a dirt road in what's call Nashville for to get an apple that somebody throw away. Even the apple was cover in dirt, Small Henry don't care, for Amen, he seen him take a big bite, swallow, and then take another big bite more.

Amen was waiting for the man he was with to

finish his whiskey in the tavern.

"'Boy!" Amen cry out. "You have yourself a good find."

Then Amen, he look at how skinny the boy was, how mess up was his thick, black hair, and his clothes, all of them, was rip and stain. And he din't have no shoes, and what Amen say, there was a chill in the air and a wind strong enough for to make the hair of his mane move. "I don't need to tell you not to waste any."

The boy take another big bite, and he din't stop staring at Amen when he done it. Then real slow like he want for to be sure, he take the apple away from his mouth, and what else, he go up to Amen and give the rest to him. "Only a donkey know what I know since I dropped screaming from my mama's belly," say the boy.

When I ask Amen, he say no, the boy wasn't afraid 'cause he tell Amen as much as he can about himself before the man got done with his whiskey. Amen find out his name and who own him and where he was at. Small Henry make Amen promise to see him again, and in a week, he did, for what happened was Amen got selled to where Small Henry was at, and that make Small Henry happy when he go down to clean the stables, and there Amen was, eating oats that was prob'ly for the horses.

Small Henry take his time for to work in the stables for Amen can tell him the story. Like me, Small Henry ask questions, and Amen answer them. But I'm not a slave, and Small Henry was, and he got to thinking why he was make to clean stables, chop wood, fetch water, and lots more than that, and he decide that he was make to believe a lie, that the fibber prob'ly had something to do with it. So one night when not even you can see the moon out, Small Henry untie Amen, and they sneak away into the woods, and what Amen say, they was as quiet and fast as two shooting stars.

They sleep when it was light out and sneak when it was dark, and Amen tell me that sometimes Small Henry, he ride Amen, for though he work like a man, he was only a boy.

Sometimes they seen people riding horses that they don't want to see—mean people with guns and chains that they believe in the fibber—but them men, they din't catch Small Henry and Amen, and them two make it where it was more safer, and that was on the north side of the Ohio, and that's a river.

"Maybe I gets to know something different," say Small Henry.

"I hope," say Amen. But then he say, "It is here I must leave you. I am going back across the river. It is there, I feel, where I should be."

The last thing Amen seen of Small Henry was him running into the woods, but right before it, Amen tell me, was apple trees with branches that they bend to the ground they had so much apples on them.

After that, there come a girl that want to be a boy and go with her dad to fight what are call Rebs. Then there was another girl that no one know her grampa, he run away from the mean men with guns and chains, too. But only this girl, she was like me and you's color. She's the one that wear all the time the hat with the big brim, and on it was tie a pink ribbon that fall down past her shoulders.

But when Amen, he was done telling her the story, and he poof away like he sometimes does, there was really nobody else till Betty Jean seen her cousin, Butchie, get hit by a car. It wasn't her fault, but maybe, she think, she could've got up from playing and run real quick and save him anyways.

Amen, he been at the farm for weeks where Betty

Jean grow up, and Amen, when he hear about Betty Jean's cousin, he whisper to her, and when she whisper back, he know it was okay for to talk out loud.

Betty Jean come to him every day after that. But after Amen, he tell her all what I tell you, that's when she say, "But I'm a big girl now."

Amen like for to spend the hot afternoons where the shade was under a sugar maple that someone leave in the pasture, so that's where he was. "I believe you want to tell me more."

"Butchie just turned three. There was a cake. I helped him blow out the candles."

"I know what happened," say Amen.

"I saw the whole thing."

"His mother shrieks at all hours, the poor child."

Betty Jean always wear dresses. Sometimes them dresses had pockets, and that's when she put her hands in them, for what her mom tell her, she had nervous hands, and it's better for to keep them in your pockets than let them move all over the place. That day, what Amen tell me, Betty Jean's hands almost burst out of her pockets. "Pretty soon, you'll be nothing but a donkey to me, and I'll go on forgetting everything you told me until I'm old and gray."

Amen bob his head up and down, which is sometimes what he does when he's thinking. Then he say, 'I don't know why your cousin went way away. It is not for any of us to know. But you know that. I told you the story."

"You told me there's nothing to fear in death."

"Yes, no more than a child should fear the embrace of a parent."

"I think that's silly," she say.

"How is that silly? We are given this peace." Amen, he stop bobbing, and now he was just looking.

Betty Jean, her hands, they just about bounce out

of her pockets right then. "When I look at my aunt,
I don't see peace. I don't *feel* peace. Where is it to be
found when a three year old gets splattered all over
the road?"

"It is ugly what happens to the body," say Amen.
"I understand."

Betty Jean sniff. "What's ugly is what we're left
with: pain, tears, endless nights. Just living is an endless
night. You told me about the fibber and how you were
spared in the desert. Holy hands."

Then what she did was laugh a little, and that
surprise Amen 'cause it wasn't happy.

But she go on, "What is hope but the peace we
can't have today?"

"Today is passing—"

"I was playing jacks. My uncle was working on
his truck across the road. Butchie was pushing himself
along on his tricycle. The road was empty. Then up over
a hill came the car, trailing dust. My aunt had walked
into the house because the phone rang."

Then's when she stop telling what happen. Amen
swish his tail onto his back like what he was trying to
get at was a thought and not a fly.

"I heard what you heard," Amen say. "The sound
was horrible, just horrible."

"How does that pass? It doesn't."

Then Betty Jean din't say nothing at all, but then
she say, "And I was just his cousin," but nothing more
after that.

"Everything is brief but God," Amen remind her.

"Brief," Betty Jean say. "When I was a little girl,
I would have believed you. But now I am big. Now I
know what I'm up against. I learned it when I watched
the wheels roll over my cousin. And in the face of
my aunt, too: terrible, ugly. Our time together is over,
Amen. It is easy for you to say that everything is brief

but God when you aren't the one being hunted."

"Hunted?"

"My body, everyone's body, will one day just stop. It may be violent, or it'll be when we're asleep. The point is that we've been abandoned to this ending, and we spend our entire lives trying to pretend we haven't. Yes, I call it being hunted. I'm no different from one of the cottontails my grandfather shoots in the field. One day an old rabbit, the next day, a baby its first time out of the nest."

So Amen, he just say, "What will you do then?"

"Run."

"In fear? Angry?"

"I have seen what God will let happen to his children," she say.

Amen, he tell me now her hands weren't moving around in her pockets no more—like they was dead and bury out of sight.

Betty Jean go on, "You told me a story, a pretty story about hope."

"I tell you the truth."

"No," she say, "not by what I've seen. But I thank you for the lie anyway. It was sweet even if I found it silly in the end."

You prob'ly know what happen next. Amen, he try to say something more, but all Betty Jean hear was *he-haw, he-haw.* She was right. She grow all big up. After that, Amen din't stay around long. He poof away for to tell the story to someone else before all what is sad and we don't know covers up the only thing we really can know.

XXX

C hirp Vanhoosen finished the story with a few thought-
ful nods, like an ellipsis, to indicate to Spring-baby
that he knew she could probably imagine for herself
the final unremarkable events that would place Amen in the
pasture about to be struck by a stone.

"I know you have a lot to do," Spring-baby said after a
moment, "with a new horse coming and all."

"I have more straw for to put down. There's food and water
I hafta get out. There's a lot to keep me busy till even after it
gets dark out."

When Chirp Vanhoosen summarily returned to the stack
of straw at the back of the barn for more bales to throw towards
the entrance of the stall he was preparing, Spring-baby took
her leave with little more than a self-conscious good-bye. She
could not explain the shame clinging to her as she left, but it
soon became no matter, for as she approached the house, that

shame slowly galvanized into a resolve to face life as it was, to avoid ducking behind vain wishes and fancy tales, to advance in age in the same manner as her elders. Perhaps she would smoke cigarettes in secret, she thought. Perhaps a butterfly would land on her arm and make sense of the whole wide world for her. She knew nothing but the soft resistance of the grass beneath her feet and the growing image of her grandparents' muffled house before her. When she reached the quick rise leading up to the front of the house, she stopped and took a deep, preparatory breath then leaned into the hill and labored upwards, around the corner, and into the house, shutting the heavy front door behind her with a resolute *thwump*.

She didn't bother to turn on any lights as she made her way to her aunt's old bedroom. Though the summer season afforded longer days, portions of the inside of the house never yielded their shadows and, therefore, had to be lit. There were no lamps or overhead lights on, however. The hallway to the bedrooms was submerged in shadows of its own creation. Not even the cracked door of her grandparents' bedroom at the end of the hallway held possibility. Spring-baby entered her aunt's old bedroom simply because it was the only thing left for her to do. She would wait for signs of life to stir. She sat on the edge of the bed and began to ponder the accessories of childhood: the dolls, the brushes, the barrettes placed neatly on the vanity.

Did Betty Jean have such items? Did she clip her hair back with a barrette the day her cousin's life was knocked out of him?

Spring-baby imagined this girl walking away from the pasture just as she had done, letting the days thicken the buffer between the past and the present. She imagined as well the prospect of growing, as Chirp Vanhoosen put it, "all big up," what that would look like, how it would feel. She tipped her head bashfully downward and studied her adolescent body. She was one of the first at school to develop, and though she was teased some when her classmates took notice, soon they too were caught up in the gradual maturation of their own bodies and were forced to scrutinize themselves instead.

After a moment, she stood up and regarded her reflection in the three-paneled mirror on the vanity. Then she placed her hands at her sides and, without thinking, sucked in her belly and pulled her slight shoulders back. She was pretty, she thought. Would she be pretty when she was older?

She relaxed her shoulders but did not turn from the mirror. Instead, she thought about Butchie, a mere baby. From the day he was born, he was destined for the grave. Just like the person in the mirror before her. Just like us all. Everyone is hunted. There is no escape.

Suddenly, Spring-baby heard the floorboards of the hallway creak. But before she could shake away the thought of being so helpless, of being death's easy quarry, Granny opened the door to Aunt Marissa's old bedroom and peered inward at her stricken granddaughter.

"I thought I heard you come in," said Granny with no trace of surprise.

"I was going to change clothes," Spring-baby uttered. "I was at the barn."

"Chirp Vanhoosen?"

"I helped him a little, and that's how I got dirty."

Spring-baby expected Granny to grunt or hum some kind of unconcerned response and leave her to get dressed, but she didn't. Rather, she stood motionless in the doorway, her hand still clutching the doorknob.

Finally, she said, "I haven't seen that donkey down there in a while. Did Chirp Vanhoosen tell you where it went?"

"He doesn't know," replied Spring-baby.

Granny released the doorknob and stuck both hands into the pockets of the dirty white bathrobe she was wearing. "That's odd," she said.

"I saw the donkey only once. Chirp Vanhoosen said the donkey probably poofed away. That's what he calls it. I don't care anymore though."

Granny said nothing for a moment, continued to stand in

the doorway, a hazy, obscure form. "You shouldn't play with smelly old donkeys anyways."

"It doesn't matter. Chirp Vanhoosen told me all about Amen. I told him I had heard enough."

"You say the donkey's name is Amen?"

"Yes."

"He poofed away, huh?"

"Yes."

Slowly, heavily, Granny pulled her hands out of the pockets of the bathrobe and took hold of the doorknob. "Silly," she said, shaking her head. "I'll make you something to eat." She pulled the door shut, leaving Spring-baby to her bleak thoughts.

Fafa walked in the door from the garage about an hour later. Granny was at the stove, spoon in hand, steam rising up around her face. Spring-baby fiddled with a napkin at the kitchen table. In complete silence, Fafa pulled out a chair and lowered himself into the seat. Only the chair itself squeaked and groaned. He stared through the table before him. Periodically, he sucked in a lungful of air and blew it out exhaustedly.

"Talked to Kevin?" said Granny without turning around.

"Not today."

"Marissa called, and we talked for about five minutes."

"Hm."

"It was warm today, what the weatherman said, but I made chili anyways."

Though the barn was a fair distance from the house, the three individuals in the kitchen could still make out the sudden *he-haw* of a donkey.

Fafa sat up a little and looked at the window. "There's that donkey Kevin doesn't like."

Spring-baby sat up, too.

"Told him stories," Fafa continued, "or that's what he pretended." He gave Spring-baby a look of mild inquisitiveness.

The donkey brayed again: a beseeching, scratchy, two-toned noise that stubbornly managed to agitate them out of their brooding.

"Chili's ready when you want it," said Granny, detectably unnerved. "Cheese is in the refrigerator." Then she left the spoon in the pot, made her way restlessly toward the bathroom, and shut the door, spraying air freshener before the final click.

"I don't care if you took a whole bushel of apples down there," said Fafa before pushing himself back up from his chair and taking his bowl to the stove.

The braying went on unabated as dark descended. Every quarter of an hour or so, the animal's call would find grandparent and grandchild alike, wherever they were, however resistant they tried to make themselves against the call. Granny cloistered herself in the bedroom while Fafa tried to hide himself in a book in a far off easy chair. Spring-baby lay tucked away in bed, her eyelids nowhere near heavy enough to give her mercy.

When finally Spring-baby was able to drift off to sleep—perhaps even inhabit some feeble, pleasant dream—the persistent *he-haw, he-haw* of the donkey would jerk her back to consciousness, forcing her again to will tranquility, hope for peace. But there was none of it. *He-haw, he-haw, he-haw* went the donkey until the wedge of light entering the room from the hallway blinked out and left the darkness absolute. Spring-baby could not sleep. She stared into the nothingness, changed position, flopped around like a fish on dry land. The braying continued unceasingly.

It was when she heard the familiar creaking of the floorboards in the hallway that she gave up trying to fall asleep altogether. At first, the creaking was lethargic, deep—some unforgiving weight pressing into the buckled tongue-and-groove planks. But quickly, surprisingly, what movement began so sluggishly grew into the unmistakable sound of someone pounding down the hallway and out of the house.

"Honey," Fafa tried sleepily, evidently trailing after his wife for the creaking sounds he, too, was making.

Spring-baby made sure she was properly clothed before opening the door to the bedroom. "What happened?" she said, peering squinty-eyed out of the open door.

Fafa was busily trying to fasten his slippers. It was after he stood up and grabbed the two ends of the cloth belt on his bathrobe that he said, "Go back to bed. Granny's upset." He started walking.

Spring-baby followed. The two wordlessly passed through the front door left open in Granny's haste. The night air was a cool, delicious swathe. The moonlight reverberated milky blue over the earth.

From the top of the rise on one side of the house, the two could easily see the glowing orange dot somewhere, Spring-baby assumed, down by the pasture fence next to the barn. From time to time, the orange dot would brighten then fall a small space where it would simmer and wait only to be lifted again, made bright, then released as if to catch its breath.

"Granny's smoking a cigarette," said Fafa needlessly.

"Fafa, what *is* that?"

It came in the beginning as an antsy yellow light that illuminated Granny's bare feet and the bottom hem of her bathrobe. But then the flickering reflections on the grass nearest the light became angrier, stabbing into the darkness, jutting upwards on Granny's small body, until the light overtook her, and she had to move back from the flames.

"What has she done?" Fafa muttered uneasily. He stood dumbstruck for only a second longer before panic finally animated his stout legs. He hurried down the small hill like a man half his corpulence.

Spring-baby watched as the blaze clawed at the roof of the barn from underneath, red and orange flames lustfully groping for any piece of virgin wood. Fire spewed and fluttered out of the windows, the door while low hanging leaves of the tree with the fat crook burned along with the nearby fence posts and the overgrown weeds around them. Granny had created her own sun. Before Fafa panted up to her, she was the only planet in its glorious orbit.

When Spring-baby saw Chirp Vanhoosen running down to the barn in what looked like nothing but a T-shirt, boots, and underwear, she sprinted down to join him.

"The barn's on fire! The barn's on fire!" he yelled, dancing confusedly around the flames, moving back when he got too close.

"Chirp Vanhoosen!" Spring-baby cried. "I heard the donkey! I heard Amen!"

But Chirp Vanhoosen either didn't hear her or chose not to, for his gaze was now securely on the two whose own focus was on the fire. "For why you catch the barn on fire?"

Granny ripped her arm away from Fafa. "Either way," she called out to Chirp Vanhoosen, "God will gain a child. It wasn't me *then*. So it had to be my son *now*."

"Betty Jean," implored Fafa, yet it was clear that she would hear none of it.

Granny eventually unlocked her glare on Chirp Vanhoosen. She was not angry with him. That, Spring-baby could tell. Granny instead turned away to gaze on the fire as if taking solace in exercising what power she could over the one with whom she *was* angry.

On and on the flames flung themselves frantically into the night sky. Spring-baby, standing apart from the others, had not let herself become mesmerized by the brilliant destruction of it all. She heard the donkey. She wanted Chirp Vanhoosen to know so.

"Hey!" she called.

But her summons was again unheeded. Chirp Vanhoosen seemed to be staring straight *into* the fire as if trying to make something out. He ventured as close to the flames as safety would permit. He looked and tried to discern, letting his mouth go agape as he puzzled over what he saw.

Spring-baby saw something also but was spared trying to figure out what it was, for suddenly bursting from the inferno came a horse as white as if it were the core of the blaze itself, tossing and swinging its head excitedly, neighing just as ferociously. The horse charged past Chirp Vanhoosen at a hard gallop, veered, then took the fence in an effortless leap, landing only feet from where Spring-baby stood. And the horse would have continued its dash, eventually vanishing into the enveloping darkness had Spring-baby not in that instant listened to impulse.

"Amen!" she yelled.

The horse halted jarringly, reared, then turned and stepped toward the girl, its breath musty-sweet as it gushed in spurts out of a massive nose.

"Let me come with you," said Spring-baby, searching the horse's glinting eyes. "I want to go where you go."

The horse snorted, pawed the ground anxiously with a powerful front hoof. Then Spring-baby finally heard the voice, and it was exactly as she had imagined.

"I go to fetch a rider," said Amen. "It will be better when I do."

"Will you come back?"

"Yes, but not alone. When I come back, you will know you were never alone. And then there will be no desire to go anywhere else again."

"Tell me, when?" she pleaded.

Amen jerked his head up in heightened alertness, for standing not far behind Spring-baby was Granny and a little bit behind her, Fafa. Each had turned their backs to the fire and were instead looking at the magnificent white steed in their midst. When Granny alone began to walk forward, Amen took his own steps to close the distance between them.

No words passed between the two, not that Spring-baby could gather at any rate from where she stood. After what seemed like mere seconds, Amen simply turned and dashed with a wild whinny across the yard, up over the hill by the house, and into the darkness, the last trace of him the energetic clippity-clop of his hooves over pavement and bare ground alike. When Spring-baby finally shifted her gaze back onto Granny, however, it was to become a long and curious study, for there Granny was, holding her heart as if some sharp object had pierced it and all she wanted to know was why.

XXXI

C hirp Vanhoosen told the firemen it had all been
an accident, for he, too, though afar, had wondered
at the white horse and imagined the blaze to be a
matter of some cosmic course he was fine in not being able
to understand. "I'm gonna build a new barn, for I need one,"
he concluded after a shrug of his bony shoulders. When
the firemen were satisfied with the work they had done
and navigated their great, lumbering red engines out of the
field, he swiftly found a shovel, placed an eight-pounder
within reach, and began the task without giving it a second
thought.

Spring-baby, though, was not around to witness. She was
holding her breath in her mother's car two hours now on the
road to Pennsylvania.

Lorelei had arrived just as the firemen below were hosing

down the very last of the flames. She had seen her daughter first, standing near the pasture fence like an apparition in a gray haze of wood smoke. Granny and Fafa were further back, the one with his arms wrapped protectively around the other. Had they watched the fire burn all night? She didn't know. She would have asked. She suffered only a look of weary disappointment from Fafa as she walked down to collect her daughter. Granny, however, paid Lorelei no mind—in fact, didn't bother to acknowledge her presence at all but instead gazed blankly, it seemed merely, at the soggy remains of what once was a simple barn.

In the end, it had taken nothing but a touch and a gesture for Lorelei to coax Spring-baby to the house where they quietly gathered Spring-baby's belongings and struck out on the long, long journey home.

"Did you find what you were looking for?" asked Spring-baby after a time. She rolled up her window the rest of the way so she would be able to hear an answer.

"Yes," replied Lorelei. "I believe I might have."

"I found something, too," Spring-baby said, her chest aching tremendously from the air stuck inside her.

"You did?"

"I did."

"Will you tell me?"

"I'll try." But the only sound that followed was the slow, peaceful escape of air over her lips—lips more supple than the day before.

Acknowledgments

It was the summer of 2006, and somewhere on a bus in China, I turned to my wife and remarked very simply that I felt I was being moved to write another book. Thank you , Geraldine, for listening ever since. You are a patient sounding board as well as a wonderful wife. My gratitude also goes out to my first readers: Anna Schachner, Jason Campbell, and Rosemary Kennevan Ashbaugh. Each of you gave me honest feedback, not generic compliments. I appreciate that, though some of it was, I confess, a bit challenging to hear. I am also grateful to Terry Kay for his continued support of my work, and to Kris McDaniel whose wisdom, unbeknownst to him, couldn't help but inform the telling of this story. Thank you, as well, to Catherine Lawton whose sensitivity and professionalism took *Gadly Plain* to a whole new level, and to Ross Boone—your drawings bring so much to the story. I am grateful to you, brother. So grateful.

–J. Michael Dew

A Conversation with J. Michael Dew

1. There have been many questions about the enigmatic title. Why did you choose Gadly Plain *and what is its significance?*

The title was discovered on a Pennsylvania back road somewhere between Interstate 80 and Warren. I was driving home from graduate school under a cloud-splotched sky, and I happened to pass one of those roads that was probably a driveway but was nevertheless given the distinction of a name: Gadly Plain. It was a rutted dirt road that more than likely led to a simple hunting camp or some far-flung place of retreat and rest. I didn't stop to inspect. Instead, I made a mental note of the catchy name, and when I pulled off the road to fish for trout further into my journey (as was my happy custom), I jotted down the name in my journal, thinking this would make a great title for a book. This was years ago. It took a lot of time since to construct my own getaway. Much of that time was spent learning why I needed to do so in the first place.

"Gadly Plain" could be "way away" or "heaven" or "paradise" or "across the rainbow bridge" or "in the bosom of God" or "Narnia." I didn't want to be too specific, thereby robbing the reader of his/her ability to imagine Gadly Plain, and I wanted to be (in my humble way) poetic. Gadly almost sounds like Godly, and the existence of heaven is a "plain" truth—nothing complicated, something a child can understand, no need for an advanced degree in theology, etc.

Have you ever seen the tractor trailers with the word YELLOW printed on the side. The word YELLOW isn't yellow at all; it's orange. That really sticks in a person's mind, right? When people see Gadly, they want to autocorrect to Gladly.

2. Most stories come directly out of the storyteller's personal experiences. Gadly Plain *is no different. What is the background of this story?*

It has been said that an early experience with death can be a good experience for a writer because the event—typically, the loss of a loved one—sparks difficult questions in the heart and mind of the bereaved that can best (so goes the wisdom) be worked out in writing. My father got sick and died when I was nine years old. To borrow a phrase from Aunt Boo, I cried borrowed tears. *Gadly Plain* amounts to one man's carefully articulated response to a boy's inexplicable trauma. There are thirty-one chapters in the book. My father was thirty-one when he died. And the maid with the German accent? She is no invention.

3. Some authors take years to write a book while others take only months. What was your process for writing Gadly Plain, *and how long did it take?*

I suppose I could say that the writing of *Gadly Plain* began the day I found out my father had passed away, but to give readers a more practical answer, one afternoon, I went out and purchased a large piece of cardstock paper on which I began to diagram plot points. The diagram grew to include characters, Biblical references, and other details I felt were important to the story. I used this diagram of sorts as an outline, keeping it in front of me each time I sat down to move the story along. All in all, it took a year to complete a first draft. Copies of that draft then went to professionals in the fields of theology, speech pathology, and creative writing. Once I got their very valuable feedback, I revised the manuscript then sent that version to another set of readers. It took a dogged effort, but it was worth it.

4. Why did you choose a talking donkey and a young man with special needs to tell the grand story of the Bible and human history?

The once-and-for-all defeat of sin and death on the cross by Jesus of Nazareth is central to what Christians believe. *Gadly Plain* is my humble attempt to echo that message, the gospel, but I wanted to do so in a disarming way. Just as the very first witnesses to the risen Lord were women (politically and socially powerless in 1st century Israel), I wanted to let this story be told to and by individuals who today might very well be considered to be socially (and certainly politically) irrelevant. All creation will be made new, and this certainly includes animals. I thought it would be interesting to get the (imagined) perspective of another species as relayed by one of the most vulnerable among us.

5. What themes are you interested in writing about next?

At least since the dawn of postmodernism, writers have largely been asserting, in various and sundry ways, the viewpoint that all values are relative, that everything is and should be deconstructed. I know I am generalizing here, but I feel this to be a safe assessment of modern literature. I believe in taking up the call issued by Wendell Berry who says that an author's duty today is to rescue some values from the dustbin of relativism and go about bravely building meaning and relevance in a world at direct odds with them both. The themes I'm interested in exploring are themes that do just that.

6. *How would you define literary fiction, and do you consider* Gadly Plain *to be categorized as such?*

I think of literary fiction in the same way that I think of classical music. Literary fiction inspires the reader to think differently about whatever topic is presented and does so without using force. In contrast, much popular fiction, as well as pop music, does little to inspire profound thought, self-revelation, epiphanies one doesn't think possible. Trash novels, and some pop music, in fact, compel the reader/listener to ape what is presented and, in the end, unwittingly participate in the steady degradation of how humans express themselves.

A work of literary fiction is a rung on a ladder leading upwards towards more dazzling, more heartfelt, more astute ways of expressing to others the complexities and nuances of this thing called the human experience. I confess that I see *Gadly Plain* as a rung. I hope others feel the same.

By no means do I want to disparage good stories (mysteries, romances, westerns, science fiction, etc.) that probably would not be classified as literary fiction. I am as fond of good stories as anybody else. I think the difference between good stories and literary fiction, though, is distinct and worth mentioning. When I choose works of fiction for the classes I teach, I choose works that can get the students to participate intellectually as well as emotionally. I believe this is what sets literary fiction apart from general fiction. With literary fiction there is a stronger pull toward intellectual engagement above and beyond mere entertainment or escapism. Of course, the deciding factors for what is and what is not literary fiction are gray. What I offer here is simply my humble opinion for what constitutes those factors.

Questions for Discussion

1. It is never articulated who the maid with the German accent is. Why? Is Dew suggesting that we need to make room for the possibility of supernatural intervention in our lives? What are your thoughts about the maid? What does her early appearance suggest about the love of God?

2. Spring-baby's first response to the news of her father's passing is to turn inward, "to stare at the abyss she didn't think possible." Is this reaction typical of anyone who learns the news of the loss of a loved one? Is her reaction heightened because of her age? If so, how? Do children respond differently to the news of the death of a close relative? What are your thoughts on Spring-baby kissing her deceased father?

3. Lorelei responds to her new widowhood by running away, presumably to collect her thoughts and emotions. Do you blame her for her response? Is she being irresponsible? Should she have gone into the viewing parlor? Is Granny being unfair with her?

4. Spring-baby's first encounter with Amen and Chirp Vanhoosen is a tense one, involving a flying rock, a struck donkey, and an incensed stable hand. Judging by what can be gleaned from Chapter IV, why does Spring-baby return to the barn and the pasture the next day? Is it shame or curiosity or something else?

5. Why is Chirp Vanhoosen's unique voice important to the story? How would the story be different if Chirp Vanhoosen were articulate or particularly well educated in theology or apologetics? What does his language pattern lend to the story?

6. Dew takes an oblique look at sin and death by noting how Amen is treated by those he encounters. They often tie him up and lash him. When Amen is about to get on the ark, Noah says that it will "be better for us all." What does Noah mean by this? Does Dew provide a fair estimation of how sin affects those who are not human?

7. What are the "butterflies" of which Lorelei speaks in Chapter X? Do you agree that we need them? Do "butterflies" come in other forms?

8. In the story, there comes a time when Uncle Kevin can no longer understand Amen. Is this development inevitable? Have we all, at one point, stopped "understanding the donkey"? Is there a way to reverse this, and if so, would we want to at all?

9. Chirp Vanhoosen says that instinct and intuition are really the same thing and that it is this faculty that lets us experience the soft nudges of God. What is the implication here for animals?

10. Spurge explains that children need a Gadly Plain because, as he says, "No kid wants to hear about God and His mysterious ways. They haven't the patience nor the ability." Do you agree? Disagree? Why? To be sure, throughout the book, heaven and the afterlife are given different names: "way away," "on an elevator," and "the good grass." Are these names helpful to understanding what happens when one passes, or are they childish? Do we need euphemisms of this sort? Does it make the reality of death less monstrous?

11. Chirp Vanhoosen is described as a "good one to listen." How is listening integral to walking well with God? How do the characters stop listening, and what are the consequences?

12. Amen characterizes humankind's actions as those born out of "the despair of broken men," not "madness." Can our social ills be explained as such? Do we do wrong because we are "broken"?

13. At the close of the book, Spring-baby is about to share with her mother what she found while staying at her grandparents' house. What do you think she'll say?

14. The overarching message of this story is one of hope. What did you, the reader, find by spending time with the characters in *Gadly Plain*? Does the message ring clear for you? Do you have stories of your own "German maid" you'd be willing to share?

About the Author

Photo credit: Sonia Biord

J. Michael Dew was born and raised in Warren County, Pennsylvania. He earned a BA in English from Lock Haven University and an MA and PhD in Literature and Criticism from Indiana University of Pennsylvania. He is an Associate Professor of English at Georgia Perimeter College where he is also the Honors Coordinator for the Dunwoody campus. He lives in Atlanta, Georgia with his wife and three daughters.

In his spare time he enjoys being a husband and a dad. And fishing. He loves a glinty, trouty stream.